GROUNDWORK GUIDES

Empire
James Laxer
Being Muslim
Haroon Siddiqui
Genocide
Jane Springer
Climate Change
Shelley Tanaka

Series Editor
Jane Springer

GROUNDWORK GUIDES

Genocide

Jane Springer

Groundwood Books
House of Anansi Press

Toronto Berkeley

To Greg and Carl

Groundwood Books / House of Anansi Press
110 Spadina Avenue, Suite 801, Toronto, Ontario M5V 2K4
Distributed in the USA by Publishers Group West
1700 Fourth Street, Berkeley, CA 94710

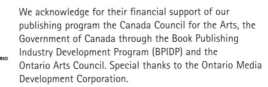

ONTARIO ARTS COUNCIL
CONSEIL DES ARTS DE L'ONTARIO

We acknowledge for their financial support of our
publishing program the Canada Council for the Arts, the
Government of Canada through the Book Publishing
Industry Development Program (BPIDP) and the
Ontario Arts Council. Special thanks to the Ontario Media
Development Corporation.

Library and Archives Canada Cataloging in Publication
Springer, Jane
Genocide / by Jane Springer.
(Groundwork guides)
Includes bibliographical references and index.
ISBN-13: 978-0-88899-681-7 (bound)
ISBN-10: 0-88899-681-0 (bound)
ISBN-13: 978-0-88899-682-4 (pbk.)
ISBN-10: 0-88899-682-9 (pbk.)
1. Genocide. 2. Genocide–History. I. Title. II. Series.
HV6322.7.S67 2006   304.6'63   C2006-902732-3

Design by Michael Solomon
Printed and bound in Canada

Contents

Chapter 1
Today's Genocide

> We know…more about the realities of ethnically targeted human destruction in Darfur than on any other previous such occasion in history. So much the greater is our moral disgrace.
>
> — Eric Reeves[1]

Bombed-out mud huts in a parched desert landscape. A two-year-old boy, face in the sand, beaten to death. Corpses stuffed into wells. An adult skeleton, wrists still tied behind its back. Anguished African women and small children in crowded refugee camps.

These images and others like them show up from time to time in the newspapers, on radio and TV. The situation in the Darfur region of Africa's largest country, Sudan, goes on and off the radar of the Western media depending on what other news is catching their attention. Meanwhile, the killing of African villagers continues.

It frequently happens in the early morning. Hundreds of *janjaweed* (armed horsemen) ride into the villages on horses or camels, their turbans covering everything except for their eyes. The Sudanese air force, in planes or helicopter gunships, have usually bombed the villages first, killing many people and scattering the rest, who are desperate to find a place to hide. Then the janjaweed, backed up by government soldiers, round up the men and boys and take them out of the village. If the hostages are lucky, the janjaweed and soldiers just shoot them. More often they torture them first. Sometimes they chain them together and burn them alive. Sometimes they behead them and throw their heads down a well to poison it for anyone left behind.

Many girls and women are kidnapped and brutally gang-raped, often in front of their families. It is common for the janjaweed to call the women "slaves" as they are raping them, shouting that now they will have Arab babies, and to mutilate or kill them afterwards.

The villages are utterly destroyed. First the janjaweed and soldiers take whatever they want — money, jewelry, food, farm animals — and then they set the huts on fire so that there is nothing for anyone to come back to. The people who do manage to escape face a dangerous hungry trek to camps that are not much safer than their homes.

Many camps lack adequate food, shelter or health care. When women and girls leave the camps to gather firewood they risk being attacked and raped by jan-jaweed waiting to terrorize them.

How It Started

Sudan's western province of Darfur is huge, the size of France. In early 2003, the largely Arab government of Sudan was confronted by a small rebel movement of African villagers in Darfur. The rebels, called the Sudanese Liberation Army, had taken up arms to protest the critical shortage of resources in Darfur and discrimination by the government in the capital, Khartoum. In response, the government turned to Arab nomads, the janjaweed, who were already often in conflict with the African farmers over their land and cattle. The government supplied arms to the janjaweed nomads and ordered them to massacre the farmers and force survivors to flee their homes. Some of these nomads are from Chad and Libya, neighboring countries badly affected by drought.

The traditional conflict between the Arabic nomads and African farmers has always been more of an economic conflict than an ethnic one. But now the Sudanese government is promoting hatred against the Africans. This is in a place where most people are Muslims and most also have dark skin, so at least for foreigners, it is hard to tell the "Arabs" and the "Africans" apart.[2]

An estimated 450,000 people from the Zaghawa, Masalit and Fur tribes have been killed or have died from starvation and disease since 2003.[3] Another 2 million of Darfur's 6 million people have been forced to flee and are living in refugee camps, 220,000 of them in Chad. Approximately 3.5 million people in Darfur are in need of food because instability in the region and the scorched earth scenario have made it impossible for them to grow any crops.

The beginning of the attacks on villages in Darfur coincided with the ending of a long war between the government and rebels in the south of Sudan. When Darfur rebels began fighting for their own rights, the government moved quickly to ensure that they were stopped before the new power-sharing government with the southern Sudanese could support Darfur.

Oil is a factor in the genocide, because even though there is no oil in Darfur itself, the Sudanese government manages to pay for its enormous military expenditures with oil. Sudan's main trading partner of oil for weapons, including tanks, aircraft, medium-sized weapons and small arms, is China. China has even helped Sudan set up its own small and medium-sized weapon production factories.

So underneath factors such as "tribal conflict" — which is often the way the Western media presents information from Africa — lie other factors such as the Sudanese government's desire to control land and regional resources and to consolidate its power.

Why Genocide?

The Sudanese government calls the situation a conflict, an attempt to put down a rebel army. According to some observers, and to the United Nations, the systematic killing, rape and destruction of people's homes in Darfur is a serious humanitarian disaster. To many other observers, however, it is a clear example of the ultimate crime against humanity — genocide.

Put simply, genocide is the systematic mass killing of a particular group of unarmed people. Although the practice is not new, the term itself is only a couple of generations old. It derives from the Greek word *genos*, which means "race" and *cide*, from the Latin verb *caedere*, which means "to kill." It was coined by the Polish lawyer Raphael Lemkin in 1943.

Genocide is a legal term with a lengthy legal definition contained in the 1948 United Nations Convention on the Prevention and Punishment of Genocide (or Genocide Convention). The concept of genocide was developed in the wake of World War II and the Nazi destruction of the Jews and Roma (or Gypsies) in order to ensure that such a crime would never take place again.

The situation in Darfur is recognized as genocide by countless individuals and non-governmental organizations and even by some governments. Documents seized from janjaweed officials clearly demonstrate the Sudanese government's genocidal intent. They urge "killing, burning villages and farms, terrorizing people, confiscating property from members of African tribes and forcing them from Darfur."[4]

Dozens of organizations have sprung up around the world to support the people of Darfur and to work to end the genocide by putting pressure on governments and the United Nations to intervene. Although the UN hesitates to call the situation genocide, in March 2005 it submitted a list of fifty-one Sudanese government and janjaweed officials to the International Criminal Court to be charged with crimes against humanity.

Yet as this book goes to press, the world community has still failed to stop the killing. The janjaweed militias have not been disarmed. In fact, their aggression has spread to eastern Chad, where they have attacked local villages and Darfurian refugee camps. Only 7,000 African Union peacekeeping troops and police have been deployed. The African Union troops do not have enough equipment to protect themselves, and they have no mandate to act against Sudanese troops and janjaweed to prevent attacks against civilians.

The work of humanitarian aid workers trying to bring some relief to Darfurian people displaced by the genocide is becoming increasingly difficult because of the general insecurity. The mortality rate from disease and malnutrition continues at 7,000 deaths per month. In April 2006, the Norwegian Refugee Council, a key humanitarian organization working in Nyala, South Darfur, was expelled from Sudan, and the head of UN operations in Darfur, Jan Egeland, was denied access to parts of the region. Direct attacks on some aid workers and a shortage of international funding for food have threatened the whole humanitarian operation.

No perpetrators of the genocide have been arrested,

much less brought to justice. In April 2006, the UN Security Council for the first time imposed sanctions (including a travel ban and a freeze on overseas assets) on four individuals involved in Darfur. But the four — an air force commander, a militia member and two rebel leaders — were of minor importance. The "big fish" were left to continue their atrocities.[5] Russia, China and Qatar abstained from the vote, signaling a likely veto if attempts are made to sanction or charge the top perpetrators of the genocide. In May 2006, a peace agreement was signed between the Sudanese government and one of three rebel groups. Not only did the agreement leave out key actors, but it had no clear peacekeeping plans to secure it, and no indication the Sudanese government would abide by it, considering its record of deceit on earlier promises to stop the atrocities in Darfur. The best that could be said of the agreement was that it was the first step in a long process that still needed forceful international commitment and intervention.

Meanwhile the media continues its sporadic, halfhearted coverage of the situation.

Never Again?

The words "never again" have been spoken many times. But the commitment that they imply — that governments and individuals everywhere will protect people in danger of becoming genocide victims and prosecute the perpetrators of genocide — has not been realized in the case of Darfur, or in many other instances of genocide that have taken place since the Genocide Convention was passed in 1948.

Why do the UN and individual countries continue to tolerate the genocide in Darfur? How does the situation there compare to other genocides in the past? Why is genocide something that most people "leave to the experts," hoping it will go away without the rest of us having to think about it? What can we do to stop the terrible cruelty and agony of genocide? How can we help prevent genocide from happening again?

This book aims to help readers answer these questions. It also hopes to honor the victims of genocide and to help ensure that their stories are not forgotten or denied.

Chapter 2
The Ultimate Crime Against Humanity

> If the killing of one Jew or one Pole is a crime, the killing of all the Jews and all the Poles is not a lesser crime.
>
> — Raphael Lemkin[1]

An everyday understanding of genocide is that it refers to the killing or attempted killing of an entire people or ethnic group. But there is plenty of debate about the definition. In fact, genocide has become a loaded word used to describe many different forms of direct and indirect killing — from the sacking of Carthage by the Romans in 146 BC to industrialized countries' current lack of commitment to provide lifesaving anti-retroviral drugs to HIV/AIDS patients in developing countries. Before taking a closer look at the definition and varying interpretations of the concept of genocide, it is worth tracking its evolution as part of the development of the wider notion of human rights.

The Evolution of Human Rights

Human rights refers to the idea that all people, whoever they are and wherever they live, have some basic rights — that is, some moral or legal entitlements — that no individual or state can take away from them. We have these rights simply because we are human.

Most scholars trace the beginnings of the contemporary concept of human rights in Western Europe and North America to the Greeks and Romans, but the first modern form to seventeenth-century England, with the 1689 Bill of Rights. The result of a long struggle between the English parliament and the monarchy, the Bill of Rights gave English propertied men certain civil and political rights and saw the end of rule by the so-called divine right of kings.[2] It was followed the next year by British philosopher John Locke's theory of people's "natural" rights to their lives, liberties and properties.

The American and French revolutions of the eighteenth century produced more comprehensive declarations of human rights. The American Declaration of Independence of 1776 recognized the fundamental rights "to life, equality, liberty and the pursuit of happiness," and the French Declaration of the Rights of Man and the Citizen of 1789 listed a set of "natural, inalienable and sacred rights" that protected citizens against the government.

The ideas behind these legal and constitutional rights took time to develop and were the product of many people's struggles against brutality and subjection. Before being taken up by politicians they were the subject of books and discussions by philosophers and other intellectuals. And although they were professed to be the rights of all citizens, many people were not considered to be citizens and were excluded from the enjoyment of these rights — workers, poor people, racial and ethnic minorities, women and children. Protection against slavery, for example, was not added to the American Constitution until 1865, almost a century after independence, and it was another hundred years before African Americans were ensured the vote with the 1965 Voters Rights Act. And in spite of the work of feminist intellectuals such as Mary Wollstonecraft, who advocated for women's equality in *The Vindication of the Rights of Woman*, published in England in 1792, the rights of "man" did not become human rights until the second half of the twentieth century.

Even for citizens whose rights were recognized, the laws were not always enforced. This was and is especially true in the case of people without money or power.

Some critics of human rights (both historic and current) contend that the concept is flawed because the lofty ideals of human rights are seldom realized in practice. Other critics, such as socialist thinker Karl Marx, see what he termed "the so-called rights of man" as fundamentally flawed because they are too individualistic, that is, based on the individual rather than on the collective, or group. This tension between the rights of the individual and the rights of the collective continues in most discussions and legal definitions of human rights today.

Numerous political struggles since the eighteenth century have been dedicated to extending the reach of human rights to encompass people without wealth or property. These struggles include workers' demands for fair wages, a shorter working day and the right to organize; the expansion of the right to vote to all of a country's citizens; the right of colonized countries to independence; and women's, racial, ethnic and religious minorities' rights to equality. In the late twentieth century, human rights activists began to focus on a broader range of rights, including the right to health, clean water, housing, education and to protection against starvation and poverty.

Crimes Against Humanity

A number of improvements on rights were made in the early twentieth century. However, it was not until the end of World War II, when the Nazis' systematic extermination of the Jews became undeniable, that a number of countries joined together and agreed to take international steps in the area of human rights.

The charter of the new United Nations, signed by forty-four countries on June 26, 1945, included a pledge of "universal respect for, and observance of, human rights." The charter also protected the right of its members to do what they wanted within their own borders and did not authorize the UN to intervene in a country's internal affairs. This commitment to the "sovereignty" of individual states continues to be a central element of international relations and a common explanation for refusing to intervene to prevent a genocide.

After the war, in 1945-46, an international tribunal was held at Nuremberg in Germany to try a number of leading Nazis under the new charge of "crimes against humanity." This term described crimes such as "murder, extermination, enslavement, deportation, and other inhumane acts committed against any civilian population, before or during the war, or persecutions on political, racial or religious grounds."[3] Although the term genocide was used during the Nuremberg Trials, it did not appear in the actual charter. But the idea had been planted, by Raphael Lemkin.

Human Rights Agreements

Following the Nuremberg Trials, United Nations initiatives continued to attempt to deal with issues raised by the war. In December 1948, the United Nations General Assembly passed two path-breaking international human rights agreements one day after another: on December 9, the Convention on the Prevention and Punishment of Genocide (the Genocide Convention) and on December 10, the Universal Declaration of Human Rights.

An Unsung Hero

Raphael Lemkin was born on a farm in eastern Poland on June 24, 1901, into a Jewish family devoted to the arts. He was educated by his mother and private tutors until he was fourteen, when he went to university. Lemkin was a gifted reader and linguist who learned to speak nine languages and read another five. Even as a child he was struck by accounts of the horrifying massacres of unarmed civilians that had taken place throughout history.

At university, first in Poland and then in Germany, Lemkin studied philology, the structure and historical development of languages. In Germany, he became interested in the trial of Soghomon Tehlirian, a young Armenian who had survived the Armenian massacres in Turkey in 1915. Tehlirian had gone to Berlin and, in 1921, assassinated one of the main instigators of the mass killings, former Turkish minister of the interior, Mehmed Talaat.

Lemkin then began to tackle the problem that became his life's work: the fact that mass killing was not punishable by law. Why, even when everyone recognized his guilt, could Talaat not be charged? Why, Lemkin asked, is it "a crime for Tehlirian to kill a man, but it is not a crime for his oppressor to kill more than a million men?"[4]

Tehlirian was acquitted and many people forgot the details presented at his trial — but not Lemkin. He began to study law and got his degree in 1929. Lemkin then worked as a public prosecutor and taught family law in Warsaw. He began preparing the draft of a law that would commit governments worldwide to outlaw and intervene in instances of mass killing.

Lemkin's proposal was presented to a conference of the League of Nations, the precursor of the United Nations, in Madrid in 1933. His suggestion was not taken up, in part because governments did not like the idea of intervening in another country's business. The Polish government frowned on his activism, so he went into private practice in Warsaw from 1934 until 1939.

When the Nazis invaded Poland in September 1939, Lemkin fled to a small town in Soviet-held Poland, where he was taken in by a Jewish family. He tried to convince them to leave because he was certain that Hitler would target the Jews. But they did not believe it could happen.

Lemkin then went to visit his parents and brother, who had gone to eastern Poland, and begged them, unsuccessfully as well, to leave with him. Lemkin escaped to Sweden, which was neutral during the war, in February 1940. He began collecting information about Nazi rule in the countries Hitler occupied.

In 1941, Lemkin left for the United States, where he taught at Duke University in North Carolina. He had no word about the fate of his family. In 1944, he published *Axis Rule in Occupied Europe*, which tirelessly lists the rules and regulations used by the Nazis and their allies (the Axis powers) to commit *genocide*. Lemkin, the superb linguist, had decided on this word to describe "a coordinated plan of different actions aiming at the destruction of essential foundations of the life of national groups, with the aim of annihilating the groups themselves."[5]

In 1946, after the end of the war, Lemkin managed to find his older brother Elias and his wife and two sons in Germany. The rest of their family had all been killed.

Naming the crime of genocide was only the beginning. Lemkin spent the rest of his life lobbying governments and diplomats to make genocide an internationally recognized crime. He was the force behind the Genocide Convention. Lemkin was nominated seven times between 1950 and 1959 for the Nobel Peace Prize, but his work was largely unrecognized, and he died in poverty in New York City on August 28, 1959.

The Universal Declaration was the first international agreement to use the term human rights and to apply human rights concepts to everyone worldwide (this is the meaning of "universal" in the title). The Universal Declaration was non-binding, meaning it had no legal force. But it was remarkable for its time — most of it is still relevant almost sixty years later — and it provided the essential groundwork, not just for hundreds of subsequent international treaties, but for the bills of rights in the constitutions of newly independent countries.

The Genocide Convention

The Convention on the Prevention and Punishment of the Crime of Genocide has the status of being the very first international human rights convention.[6] In article 1, the signing governments "confirm that genocide, whether committed in time of peace or in time of war, is a crime under international law which they undertake to prevent and to punish." In article 2, genocide is defined as committing any of the following acts "with the intent to destroy, in whole or in part, a national, ethnic, racial or religious group":

    a. Killing members of the group;
    b. Causing serious bodily or mental harm to members of the group;
    c. Deliberately inflicting on the group conditions of life calculated to bring about its physical destruction in whole or in part;

What Rights Do We Have?

Knowing our rights is the first step in ensuring that they are not ignored. Here's a brief summary of the rights set out in the Universal Declaration of Human Rights. Everyone, "without distinction of any kind, such as race, color, sex, language, religion, political or other opinion, national or social origin, property, birth or other status," has the right to:

- life, liberty and security of person
- not be in slavery
- not be subjected to torture or to cruel, inhuman or degrading treatment
- recognition before the law
- not be subjected to arbitrary arrest, detention or exile
- a fair and public hearing
- freedom of movement
- a nationality
- marry, with free and full consent of both people
- own property
- freedom of thought, conscience and religion
- freedom of opinion and expression
- freedom of peaceful assembly and association
- work and to join trade unions
- rest and leisure
- an adequate standard of living
- education

d. Imposing measures intended to prevent births within the group;
e. Forcibly transferring children of the group to another group.

Article 3 states that "conspiracy to commit genocide" is also against the Genocide Convention, as are "direct and public incitement to commit genocide," "attempt to commit genocide" and "complicity in genocide." So it is not necessary to kill people to commit the crime of genocide — planning genocide or encouraging or persuading others to commit genocide are also crimes, as are preventing a group's reproduction or forcibly removing children from their families.

The phrase "in whole or in part" indicates that it is not necessary to kill all the members of a group for a crime to qualify as genocide. And while there is no stated minimum number of people who must be killed for an act to be defined as genocide, the definition most commonly applies to situations of mass murder.

The fact that the definition of genocide includes both the element of intent and any of the particular five acts (a. to e. above) causes confusion and some controversy, especially over the determination of what exactly constitutes intent and how intent can be proven. Is intent only verifiable from written documents or recorded statements outlining plans to exterminate a group? Or can intent also be implied when a government or group engages in a systematic pattern of actions — such as forced marches leading to death by starvation and disease — that would clearly have the effect of killing off a group? Genocide specialists are leaning toward the broader definition, as we shall see in the discussion of genocide and colonialism in the next chapter.

The convention's definition of genocide was not as extensive as Lemkin and others had hoped, especially because it does not include the deliberate killing of political and social groups. The UN definition, therefore, does not include the mass killing of "enemies of the people" in the Soviet Union in the 1930s or the massacre of "communists" in Indonesia in the 1960s or the killing of social groups such as homosexuals or the disabled, both of whom were targeted by the Nazis, along with the Jews and the Roma. (Organizations of social groups could of course also be termed political groups.)

The original draft of the Genocide Convention definition did include crimes that were committed for political reasons. However, the inclusion of "political groups" was rejected by the Soviet Union. The original draft also included references to "cultural genocide" (as opposed to "physical" genocide), which was opposed by Canada and other Western countries.[7] Like all international agreements, the Genocide Convention was a product of numerous concessions and compromises made to protect the interests of individual countries.

The passing of the Genocide Convention was nevertheless a ground-breaking achievement and a high point in the history of human rights. Regrettably, the convention was scarcely used in the decades following World War II.

Chapter 3
A History of Mass Violence

> The Rwandan genocide needs to be thought
> through within the logic of colonialism.
> — Mahmood Mandami[1]

Once the "crime of crimes" had been named by Raphael
Lemkin, scholars began to look for genocide in earlier
periods of history. What is horrifying is that they found
it almost everywhere. It had a somewhat different
appearance in the past, however. The main difference
between earlier instances of genocide and modern genocide is that it used to be a more acceptable part of conquest, something to be proud of, and nothing to hide.
Genocide scholar Roger W. Smith points out that with
the development of the concept of human rights, the
killing off of an entire people was not so easily morally
justified, and in the nineteenth and twentieth centuries,
genocidal activities tended to become hidden.[2]

There is no consensus among genocide scholars about
when the earliest genocides occurred. It seems clear,

however, that genocide did not begin in the hunting and gathering stage of human history, when people lived in small groups and were widely dispersed, but some time after the discovery of agriculture. It was once people developed agricultural surpluses, a form of wealth, and engaged in trade and began to set up cities and armies that the first instances of genocide probably took place.[3]

The Bible recounts several genocides committed in the name of God, including the story of Joshua and the extermination of the Canaanites in Jericho. The complete destruction of Carthage by Rome in 146 BC, after a three-year siege, is another of the first-known genocides. An estimated 150,000 people out of a total population of 200,000 were killed, and Carthaginians living in other regions were never allowed to return to the site of the city. It is not clear whether the Romans killed all the survivors of the siege, intending to exterminate them, or whether the citizens died from hunger or sickness. But in any case, the Carthaginians "vanished from history" as genocide historians Chalk and Jonassohn put it.[4]

Many other peoples have also vanished from history, with little or no historical explanation, perhaps as a result of genocide. We don't know for sure, because the history of genocide is largely unrecorded. Why? In part because history is always written by the victors, the ones who remain. And in part because people often want to bury the past, to put traumatic events out of their minds or "turn a blind eye," so that they don't have to think about them.

The Victors Write the History

People who are vanquished don't usually get a chance to tell their side of the story. They're either dead, or they're afraid of being killed or persecuted, or they don't have the power or the status or the means of communication to get their stories out. Survivors sometimes feel guilty about the very fact of surviving. Why me? they ask. They don't want to draw attention to themselves or relive their stories. Sometimes it takes centuries for their stories — or the full story — to be told. It usually takes even longer for the story to be listened to and acknowledged and accepted.

This is true of the history of colonialism, which is the extension of one country's power to other lands and peoples, and the settlement of and control over that land and people. It is only in recent decades, for example, that North and South American history books have questioned the "discovery" of America by Christopher Columbus and have begun to acknowledge the immense human consequences of the colonization of aboriginal peoples by the Europeans.

The same is true in Africa, where hard-won struggles for independence over the last half century have finally allowed African historians to begin to tell the continent's history, including the history of slavery and the slave trade, from African points of view.

These new histories demonstrate a strong link between colonialism and genocide. The imperialist powers had superior military strength and were able to kill large numbers of subjected people who were occupying the land they wanted. In most parts of the world, indigenous people were dehumanized by the colonizers and termed "backward" or "savages," which somehow justified killing them and destroying their culture. In some places, such as the Congo in Africa, torture and massacres were carried out to terrorize people into forced labor. Adam Hochschild estimates that half the population of 20 million Congolese were killed between 1880 and 1920, the majority during the twenty-three-year rule of King Leopold of Belgium, which started in 1885.[5]

In 1904 in Southwest Africa (now Namibia), German colonialists pushed the Herero people off their land to make way for German settlers. The Hereros fought back, and in retaliation the colonialists massacred thousands, driving the rest into the desert. Any who tried to escape were killed. Most starved to death, and the Hereros were virtually exterminated — about 64,000 of a population of 80,000.

The colonial conquest and killing of the Hereros is generally accepted as genocide. After all, the written instructions from Berlin ordering the German army to exterminate the Hereros still exist today.[6] There is not the same consensus about using the term genocide to describe other colonial situations. Many specialists claim that in North, Central and South America, Australia and New Zealand, the annihilation of indigenous people is not genocide because the people were not killed intentionally, but were wiped out by a combination of killing, disease and starvation. The killing and/or dying off of whole tribes is often seen as a mere fact of life, something that just happened as part of "progress." But this passive point of view is a kind of denial, a refusal to acknowledge what really happened, and perhaps especially to accept any responsibility for what took place.

The evidence, some of it written by the colonizers themselves, some of it passed down orally among survivors, demonstrates countless examples of genocidal activities, including dehumanization of the native peoples, extermination, mass murder, torture, rape, forced marches to poorer land, and taking children from their parents.

The Genocide of Native Americans

The European conquest of North and South America is "the most massive interrelated sequence of genocides in the history of the world," according to historian David Stannard. From Columbus' arrival in Española (now the Dominican Republic and Haiti) in 1492 until the massacre by the US Army at Wounded Knee in 1891, an unimaginable 95 percent of North American native people were killed or died.[7]

This five-hundred-year series of genocides includes the conquest of the Aztecs in what is now Mexico and the complete extinction of the Arawaks/Tainos in the Caribbean and the Beothuks in Newfoundland. It includes evidence that on at least one occasion British authorities intentionally distributed blankets or other items infected with smallpox to the native people in what is now the United States. It includes forced re-locations, internments and marches, such as the Trail of Tears in 1838-39, when the Cherokees were forcibly evacuated from their land east of the Mississippi River to make way for white settlement. The Cherokees were driven from their homes at gunpoint and kept in intern-ment camps before being led on the forced march. Almost a third of the 15,000 Cherokees died from star-vation or disease.

The more recent practice in the US and Canada (as well as in Australia and New Zealand) of sending aborig-inal children to residential boarding schools has also been called genocide, according to the Genocide Convention's inclusion of the forcible transfer of children. The schools in these countries were characterized by overcrowding and inadequate food and medical care, and many chil-dren died from starvation and disease. Sexual violence and rape were also common in the schools.

All of these practices are included in the Genocide Convention's definition of genocide. The only difficulty for some is the question of intention. They argue that because there was no overall plan to wipe out native peoples in what is now Mexico, for example, that it cannot be termed genocide. Others argue that there is nothing to say that intention must be directly stated or acknowledged. People often do things "without thinking" or "without meaning to," only later realizing (or perhaps always denying) that they intended to do them all along. It is also easy to take the first steps in a process that is later difficult or impossible to stop. But if the pattern is there and it is recognizable, it cannot continue to be denied. Genocide specialist Roger W. Smith points out that:

Sometimes…genocidal consequences precede any conscious decision to destroy innocent groups to satisfy one's aims.…With the recognition of the consequences of one's acts, however, the issue is changed: to persist is to intend the death of a people.[8]

Sooner or later, European descendants in the Americas must face the fact of their own genocidal history and begin the lengthy and needed process of reconciliation with native peoples. Otherwise, indigenous communities from the north of Canada to the southernmost tip of South America will continue to be the poorest and most disadvantaged communities of the Americas, whose basic human rights to land and to their

THE ARMENIAN GENOCIDE

Armenians, a predominantly Christian minority in the chiefly Muslim Ottoman Empire, were discriminated against but had generally lived peacefully in the southern Caucasus region (between the Black and Caspian Seas), for over two thousand years. The situation changed in the nineteenth century as the seven-century-old Ottoman Empire began to break down. (The Ottoman Empire was founded by Turkish tribes in Anatolia in the thirteenth century. What is now Turkey formed only part of it, but the Ottoman Empire was often called Turkey even before the republic was officially declared in 1922.)

Corrupt, badly administered and lagging behind Western capitalist development, the Ottoman Empire, with its capital in Constantinople (now Istanbul) faced a number of regional revolts.

As nationalist sentiments burgeoned throughout the empire, the Armenians began their own cultural revival, demanding regional autonomy and other human rights. This movement was suppressed by Ottoman sultan Abdul Hamid II from 1894 to 1896, when 200,000 Armenians were killed in massacres.

When the "Young Turks," a group of army officers, overthrew the sultan in 1908, the Armenians at first rejoiced, but their situation worsened. The sultan had attempted to keep Armenians "in their place," but three new leaders in 1913 — Enver Pasha, Jemal Pasha and Talaat Pasha — were militant nationalists who began to plan the extermination of the Armenian population.

The opportunity to proceed with the genocide took place during World War I, which pitted Germany, Austria-Hungary and Turkey against the Allies, including Britain (and then-colonies India, Canada, Australia and New Zealand), France and Russia. Armenians lived on both sides of the Russian-Turkish border and pleaded with Turkey not to go to war against Russia. When asked to organize an insurrection against the Russians in the Caucasus, the Armenians refused. The Turks then accused the Armenians of supporting the Russians and branded them as traitors.

On the night of April 24, 1915, six hundred prominent Armenian men — community leaders, intellectuals, professionals and businessmen — were pulled from their homes and taken away to be shot. Armenian men in the Ottoman army had already been stripped of their weapons and forced into being laborers. Now those who had not died from overwork, illness or starvation were taken out in groups and shot, falling into graves they had just been forced to dig.

The rest of the Armenian population was told that they were being deported to other countries. Adult and teenaged men were quickly separated from the women, the children and the elderly and were shot. The women, children and old people were driven from their homes by soldiers and forced to walk for weeks without food. The girls and women were attacked — tortured, raped and often killed — by soldiers, peasants, villagers or prisoners who had been released to assist in the genocide. Some women were offered the chance to survive if they married a Turk and converted to Islam. Many women committed suicide by throwing themselves and their children off cliffs or into rivers.

Estimates of the number of Armenians killed range from 1.1 million to 1.8 million — between one-half and three-quarters of all Ottoman Armenians.

Was the Slave Trade Genocide?

An estimated 12 to 15 million Africans were taken to colonies in North America, South America and the Caribbean islands between 1500 and 1850 to be used as slaves. These were the people who survived. David Stannard estimates that between 36 and 60 million men, women and children died *before* they ever started work as slaves in the "New World."[9] Huge numbers died on forced marches to the west African coast or in the horrific holding pens where they were imprisoned before boarding ship. Many died on the ships themselves, from malnutrition or disease, and many more died within the first year of reaching their destination.

The slave traders and owners did not intend to exterminate the Africans, but to use them as unpaid workers. As could have been foreseen, however, cruel treatment, wretched living conditions and disease killed millions of people. The slave trade was recognized as a crime against humanity by the 2001 World Conference against Racism in Durban, South Africa. The conference could have gone further and acknowledged that even if not directly intended, the mass killing or dying off of African slaves was genocide.

own language, to education and justice, as well as to freedom from discrimination, brutality and even torture continue to be violated.

Turning a Blind Eye

When people are faced with an uncomfortable truth or feeling — one that threatens their world view or their sense of themselves — they often deny knowledge of the truth or deny ever having the feeling. Denial can happen at the level of the individual or collectively, at the level of a whole society or a government or groups of governments.

The condition of denial is sometimes described in terms of "not seeing" or blindness. People are described as "wearing blinkers" or "turning a blind eye" or "sticking their heads in the sand." Or denial may be described as "not speaking," as silence.

Clearly, some statements of denial are perfectly correct — no crime has been committed. Other denials are revealed to be outright lies. But in still other cases, the situation is not clear, or the real truth is unknown, or our minds block out the real truth as a defense against the horror that acknowledging it (or even more difficult, accepting responsibility for it) would bring.

A clear example of a genocide that has been denied by governments, even when the facts were known, is that of the Armenians by the Ottoman Empire (now Turkey) in 1915. Chapter 5 considers the denial by individuals actually involved in a genocide — as perpetrators, bystanders or victims.

The Denial Continues

The details of the Armenian genocide were left out of most Turkish history books and "forgotten" for decades. The Turkish government succeeded in convincing many people and governments that the story of the genocide was a lie. Adolf Hitler himself took advantage of this

THE FORCED FAMINE IN UKRAINE

Ukraine, a fertile region where 80 percent of the population were peasant farmers, declared itself independent after the 1917 Soviet revolution. Independence lasted only until 1921, when it became a Soviet republic. Ukrainians were the largest minority group in the USSR, but at the end of World War I, western parts of Ukraine were given to Poland, Romania and Czechoslovakia. Starting in 1929, 5,000 Ukrainian religious and cultural leaders and intellectuals were accused of revolting against the state and arrested. Some were shot; others were deported to prison camps.

Ukrainian peasants resisted giving up their farms to the "collectivization" demanded by the Soviet government. It involved the establishment of huge industrial state-owned farms where the peasants no longer had control of their land or crops. Part of the process involved a campaign by Stalin and the Soviets against the *kulaks*, supposedly wealthy farmers who owned more than ten hectares (twenty-four acres) or who employed other workers. In fact, kulaks were more likely to be those resisting forced collectivization. At least 5 million people were sent to the Russian Arctic, where it was impossible to farm, and they died by the thousands.

Over the next few years, the Soviet state required the Ukrainian collective farms to produce unrealistic amounts of grain. When, because of transportation problems or a poor harvest, the quotas were hard to meet, the state still insisted on the quotas being fulfilled, leaving little for the peasants, now workers, to eat. By 1932, the collective farms had stopped providing food to the peasant workers. To ensure that they didn't take grain from the farms, a new law made death the penalty for stealing food. Starving people who were caught with even a fistful of grain were shot on the spot. Meanwhile, much of the abundant wheat crop was being sold outside the country to pay for Soviet industrial projects and the military.

Ukrainian communist leaders protested the situation, asking for a reduction in the grain quotas and for food aid. Instead, the military moved in Russian soldiers, sealed the borders of Ukraine and prevented food and goods from entering. Three million people left their homes, looking for food. They couldn't go north to Russia because of the blockade. Some managed to get to the Ukrainian capital, Kiev, but even there, there was little food. People ate anything they could find — leaves from trees and bushes, birds, cats, dogs, even other people, in some cases. In the spring of 1933, people were dying at the rate of 25,000 per day.

The state continued to block the border and to refuse to send food to people in Ukraine. It denied that the forced starvation was taking place. Even uttering the word "famine" was against the law, and anyone who did so could be arrested and killed.

An estimated 7 million people, including 3 million children — almost all of them peasants — died in the winter of 1932-33. One-quarter of the population of Ukraine was killed.

Relief was finally sent in the summer of 1933. By this time both the kulaks and the Ukrainian resistance had been destroyed. Grain quotas were decreased and existing stocks were used to feed the peasants.

The forced famine was denied by the USSR and ignored by other governments who used the excuse of not interfering in a country's internal affairs. It was only with the opening up of the Soviet Union in the mid-1980s that the story began to be told openly.[10]

denial of history. In 1939, urging his generals to be brutal in their invasion of Poland, he said, "Who today remembers the extermination of the Armenians?" In other words, the Turks got away with it; so can we.

This denial of the Armenian genocide continues today. Some Western governments allied with Turkey have, against Turkey's wishes, finally acknowledged the fact of the genocide. But Turkey itself still refuses to admit it. Not only does Turkey censor discussion of the genocide, but those Turks who speak openly about it may face criminal charges. Charges against award-winning novelist Orhan Pamuk for insulting Turkey, because of his acknowledgment of the genocide, gained worldwide attention in late 2005. The charges were dropped in early 2006, just before the European Union was to review the Turkish justice system, part of the process of Turkey's bid to join the EU.

Other examples of long-denied genocides are those that took place during the period of state terror and mass violence in the Soviet Union, including the Ukrainian famine of 1932-33 (see pages 38-39). Of course, the more individuals and governments are able to get away with denial, the easier it is for genocide to recur and for it to be denied again and again.

Chapter 4
Theories of Genocide

> What we learned from Rwanda is that the worst inhumanity we can imagine will come again. If there's a lesson, it is that having seen it before doesn't immunize us. The opposite may be true: the more we see it the more we accept it as part of our condition.
>
> — Philip Gourevitch[1]

While the actual naming of genocide has allowed genocide scholars to see the similarities in mass killings across the centuries, every genocide is different. Every genocide arises from a complex set of situations that makes it unique. Recognizing that every genocide takes place under very specific conditions, genocide scholars have nevertheless identified a number of theories about why, when, where and how genocide takes place.

Why Does Genocide Take Place?
Most people are acquainted with the "one evil man" view

of genocide. The most common example attributes the Nazi extermination of the Jews and Roma to Adolf Hitler alone. Another infamous example is Saddam Hussein, who is often single-handedly credited with the massacre of between 50,000 and 200,000 Kurds in northern Iraq in 1988. Yet while Hitler and Saddam were undoubtedly the key decision-makers in these genocides, they could not have carried them out themselves. This theory does not explain how hundreds, thousands or even millions of people in a society are drawn into participating in a genocide. And it does not take into account or investigate the political, economic and social situations that might lead to genocide.

Genocide specialists have developed more complex theories. They point out that although it may seem to arise suddenly, with no warning, genocide does not take place without extensive preparation and planning on the part of the instigators or perpetrators. In their own minds, the perpetrators have good reasons for wanting to get rid of a particular group of people. This is not to say, of course, that these reasons are justified or make sense.

In some cases, a government or an influential group wants new settlers to take over the land of the people already living there. This was the case with the Hereros in southern Africa and the Beothuks in Newfoundland, Canada. Or a government or group or corporation may want to develop an area where indigenous people live — that is, extract resources like lumber or minerals, build a dam or set up a factory. This is the case with the ongoing extermination of indigenous groups in parts of South America. In Colombia in 2005, for example, 3,000 indigenous people and Afro-Colombians were killed by US-backed soldiers or militias and another 300,000 displaced in government attempts to push them off lush farmland and areas rich in minerals. While this situation has not been recognized as genocide per se, it is dangerously close.

In other cases, a group or a government feels threatened by another ethnic, political or social group and wants to ensure its control over a nation by getting rid of the offending group. This is part of the complex rationale for the Rwandan genocide, where the majority Hutus, who were in power, committed genocide against the minority Tutsis.

In still other genocides, a government wants to set up a society that it sees as "perfect" or utopian, one where only people of a certain race or class or religion or sexual orientation will be allowed to live. Many genocide leaders say they are "cleansing" or "purifying" their nation of the "contaminating influence" of "rats" or "cockroaches." Both the Holocaust and the Cambodian genocide are examples of this motive. And, of course, these motives are often related. For example, the motive of wanting to ensure control is often linked to wanting a rigid, undifferentiated society where only certain types of people are deemed to be true citizens.[2]

Where Does Genocide Take Place?

Genocides can and do take place anywhere and everywhere (see Genocides through History, pages 120-25). Societies that promote very nationalistic ideas, that glorify their own nation and revile others, that are not open to diversity of thought and religion and expression are more likely to be places where genocide can occur. The break-up of the Soviet Union, for example, resulted in the collision of a number of nationalist movements within the former Yugoslavia.

Another place where genocide appears more likely to occur is in a place where the perpetrators have themselves been victims of violence or genocide in the past. This may be one factor in the Rwandan genocide. In 1972 the Hutus had been victims of genocidal massacres by the Tutsis in neighboring Burundi. And in 1994 Hutus killed a million Tutsis in Rwanda.

When Does Genocide Take Place?

Genocide often takes place during a time of war, or more accurately, under the cover of war. War is often used to mask or cover up a genocide. The Armenian genocide and the Holocaust are both examples of genocides that took place while the Ottoman Empire and Germany, respectively, were waging war with other countries.

Wartime acts against civilian enemies, such as the Allied bombing of Hiroshima and Nagasaki during World War II, have been termed genocide by some writers. While many agree that these bombings were war crimes, the intent was not to destroy an entire group or a substantial portion of it, but to end a war. Genocide specialist Roger Smith, however, points out that nuclear war, which could potentially wipe out all of the human race as well as all other life on earth, would be the ultimate genocide, an "omnicide."[3]

Genocide is often described by the perpetrators as part of a civil war, or a war between armed factions within a country. But again, this is usually just an excuse for killing the victims with impunity (i.e., without being punished). The government claims that it is defending the national state by "fighting" with the victims, who are unarmed. This has happened in Darfur. Civil war is also used as a reason for not intervening to help the victims: "Oh, it's a fight between opposing groups inside the country, it's none of our business." Because although genocide as defined in the convention merits intervention, civil war does not. Similarly, a government may call the victims terrorists or supporters of terrorists in order to justify killing them.

If it does not occur during wartime, a genocide often takes place during a period of political or social upheaval. Genocide expert Helen Fein identifies as a possible candidate for genocide a society that is moving from being authoritarian to being more democratic, a situation that frequently sets off a struggle for power.[4]

Genocide may also take place in a situation where the

Racism and Genocide

Racism is a set of attitudes and practices that believes in the natural superiority of one "racial group" or cultural or ethnic group over another. This term is commonly used to describe beliefs and practices that discriminate against a particular group because of physical characteristics such as skin color, even though there are no separate races of human beings. All humans belong to the same species — the human race.

Ethnocentrism is sometimes used to describe attitudes and practices that elevate one ethnic or cultural group above another. Both racism and ethnocentrism generally involve discrimination that leads to mistreatment or even dehumanization of outsider groups, which may then lead to genocide.

Racism may cause genocide. It may also be a reason for allowing a genocide to continue. Major Brent Beardsley, who worked with General Romeo Dallaire in Rwanda, argues that the lack of response to the genocides in Rwanda and Darfur suggest that Western "white" governments do not consider the death of an African to be equal to the death of a white person.[5]

state has solidified its power. Gregory Stanton of Genocide Watch argues that genocides do not result from "state failure," but from "state success, from too much state power."[6] This was the case in Nazi Germany, in the Soviet Union in the 1930s and in Cambodia in the 1970s, for example.

How Does Genocide Take Place?

There are conflicts between people in most societies, and in most societies, there are people who hate other people or want to have power over them. They may focus this hatred on people's characteristics — on their race, their ethnic background, their class, their religion, their sexual orientation or even their gender. In most cases, this hatred and people's vengeful, even murderous thoughts are not acted upon. In some cases, however, people develop elaborate theories to explain what they see as differences between groups and begin to act and encourage others to act against the reviled groups. When a large part of a society is caught up in acting upon — or ignoring others acting upon — these hatreds, the situation may become a genocide.

THE HOLOCAUST

The genocide of the Jews and Roma by Hitler's Third Reich has come to be known as the Holocaust, with a capital H. The term holocaust, which comes from ancient Greek, originally meant a sacrifice burned on an altar. Its current meaning, with a lower-case h, is "destruction or slaughter on a mass scale."[7]

The persecution and killing of other targeted groups — including Slavic peoples (Poles and Russians), the mentally and physically disabled, leftists (socialists, social democrats, Marxists and communists), homosexuals, Afro-Germans and Jehovah's Witnesses — although not so well known, are also part of the Holocaust.

It was evident from the early 1930s that the Third Reich's fascist policies intended harm against a number of groups. Adolf Hitler's *Mein Kampf* (My Struggle), first published in 1925, clearly states his thinking: he hated Jews and leftists, whom he saw as one and the same (i.e., all Jews were leftists and all leftists were Jews);[8] the German Aryan blond-haired, blue-eyed "race" was superior and the Slavs were inferior; Germans needed *Lebensraum* or "living space" (in effect, other countries' territory), and they needed a leader who had absolute authority.

The Genocide of the Jews

Hitler and the National Socialist German Workers' Party, or Nazis, came to power in Germany in January 1933. A month later, they suspended a number of constitutional rights, including the rights to personal liberty, free expression, freedom of the press and the rights of assembly and association. In October, Germany quit the League of Nations, the forerunner of the United Nations.

Trade unions were abolished. A series of anti-Jewish laws were decreed, prohibiting Jews from owning property or working at professional jobs. Anti-Semitism was not new in Europe, but it took on a more virulent form under the Nazis.

The Nazis began humiliating, terrorizing and arresting Jews, especially Jews who were also leftists. The Nazis controlled the media, the arts, science and education. Books by Jews or ones that were considered "dangerous" or contrary to Aryan ideals were publicly burned. Textbooks were rewritten and replaced. Beggars, the homeless and the unemployed were sent to concentration camps under a new law against "habitual and dangerous criminals." In August 1934, Adolf Hitler became the Führer or "absolute ruler" he had foreseen in *Mein Kampf*.

The number of Jews in Germany at the time Hitler came to power is estimated at 505,000, less than 1 percent of the total German population of 67 million. Their ancestors had lived in Germany for hundreds of years and they spoke German. Although the Nazis wanted to get rid of the Jews, it appears that at first they were trying to get them to leave Germany, not necessarily to kill them all. And the Jews themselves either thought the Nazis would soon be out of power, or because they saw themselves as German did not believe their situation would worsen, or they had nowhere to escape to. Emigration was difficult because of anti-Semitism and the resulting strict entry requirements in other countries. A small percentage of Jews — about 7 percent, an estimated 37,000 people — did leave Germany in 1933, however.

By September 1935, Jews had lost their citizenship and could not marry non-Jews. Anti-Semitism was official policy. The Nazis tried to cover up their racist policies during the Olympics, which were held in Berlin in August 1936. When Hitler annexed Austria in March 1938, Austria's 200,000 Jews were immediately deprived of their rights and property. The persecution that had been gradually intensifying in Germany was quickly instituted in Austria.

On November 9, 1938, a young Jewish man, Herschel Grynszpan, shot a German official at the embassy in Paris to avenge his parents, who had been forcibly returned to Poland from Germany. The Nazis used the death of the official, Ernst vom Rath, as an excuse for carrying out a massacre of Jews in Germany. During *Kristallnacht* (the Night of the Broken Glass), Nazi storm troopers and gangs set over a hundred Jewish synagogues on fire. They ran through Jewish neighborhoods attacking people, breaking windows in homes and destroying and looting shops. Ninety-one people were killed, 7,500 businesses damaged or destroyed and 30,000 Jewish men arrested and sent to concentration camps.

World War II started in September 1939 with the German invasion of Poland. By then, more than 200,000 Jews had left Germany, and the Nazi government had seized any property they had left behind. This money propped up the Nazi regime and helped buy the compliance of the German people in the mass killing of the Jews.

Poland had the largest Jewish population in Europe, over 3 million people. Jews in Poland were required to wear badges on their left chests with the yellow Star of David on them. This had the effect of clearly dividing citizens into Jews and non-Jews.

They were soon forced into walled ghettos in the worst areas of cities where overcrowding, starvation and disease began to kill thousands. In the Warsaw Ghetto, for example, the food allotment was only 181 calories a day. People either managed to smuggle in food or they died.[9]

In April 1940, the Nazis invaded Denmark and Norway, and in May, France, Belgium, Holland and Luxembourg. The Jewish people living in all these countries, some of whom had fled Germany in order to escape Nazi rule, were now under Hitler's control.

Most historians agree that mid-1941 marked a turning point in the Holocaust — the point where the decision to wipe out the Jews was made. As he was about to invade the Soviet Union, Hitler told his generals that the coming "war of annihilation" would target communists and Jews. Special mobile killing units known as *Einsatzgruppen* were sent in to round up and murder Jews, Poles and Soviets. Jews were no longer allowed to emigrate. People were taken in the thousands to areas outside towns, forced to undress and then shot into pits or graves that they had dug themselves. In just two days in September 1941, 35,000 Jews were massacred in a ravine at Babi Yar, outside the Ukrainian city of Kiev.

The Nazis began to talk about the "Final Solution of the Jewish Problem." Although they continued to shoot Jews in some areas, the Nazis constructed special killing centers with gas chambers. All the Jews of Europe were to be rounded up and sent to six main camps in Poland. Belzec, Chelmno (Kulmhof), Sobibor and Treblinka were extermination camps. Auschwitz-Birkenau and Majdanek had both work camps and gas chambers. Younger adults, mainly men and some women, were chosen to work. Others, including most children, their mothers, pregnant women and the elderly, were sent directly to the gas chambers. Many thousands were worked to death. The few who survived did so with a combination of luck and determination.

Germany had varying degrees of control over the Jewish population in the countries it occupied. The fate of Jews depended on how each country responded to German demands to deport them to the camps. The Nazis emphasized that the countries could keep all Jewish goods and property. Most countries, including France, Greece, Hungary, the Netherlands, Poland and Norway, rounded up their Jews and deported them to the camps, although some individuals in these countries hid and protected Jews. Some countries, like Denmark, Finland, Italy and Romania, refused to hand them over, and so in these countries, most Jews survived.

Millions of men, women and children were transported by train

Genocide by Assembly Line

Ghettos, concentration camps, forced marches, mass executions, death by starvation and disease were common elements of earlier genocides. The Nazis added a new technological dimension to genocide. The gas chambers were only one step in an elaborate assembly line beginning when the Jews were hustled, one car at a time, out of packed and stifling freight trains. They were quickly separated into two groups — those to work and those to be killed immediately. The second group was led into a large room or to an outdoor area where they were told to undress for bathing and de-lousing. In some camps, the women's hair was cut. The people were then funneled into the gas chambers.

The assembly line didn't end with the victims' death: it continued as fellow prisoners, belonging to a special detail, cleared out the bodies and carted them to a nearby crematorium. In some of the camps, the special-detail men were forced to extract the gold from the corpses' teeth before shoving them into the fire. Everything was used: the gold, the victims' hair, their clothes, even their ashes, which were spread on the fields. A trainload of people disposed of in under three hours.

to the camps from all over Europe, but chiefly from northern, western and central Europe. Most of the Jewish population of eastern Europe was killed in mass shootings by troops and militia.

Six million Jews were killed before the end of the war in April 1945, more than two-thirds of the 8.9 million Jews in Europe. Three million were killed by gas in the death camps, almost two million were shot, and a million died of overwork, starvation and disease.

The Genocide of the Disabled

In accordance with the desire for a pure Aryan race, in mid-1933 a new Nazi law forced the sterilization of people with so-called hereditary diseases. The idea was that people who the Nazis thought were not perfectly healthy should not be allowed to have children. The law affected the mentally and physically disabled, including the deaf, alcoholics and people with physical deformities and epilepsy. Most of the 300,000 to 400,000 people sterilized were in institutions.

In 1939, a Hitler decree allowed doctors to kill "patients considered incurable" under the "euthanasia" program. The Nazis mis-used the term euthanasia or "mercy killing." The patients were not asking to die and the killing, originally by lethal injection, was done in secret. Later, carbon monoxide gas was used, killing the disabled with a procedure that soon would be used in the gas chambers.

German children born with disabilities were among the first to be killed. Mental patients in occupied territory, especially in Poland, Russia and East Prussia, were also killed, either by the *Einsatzgruppen* or by gas. There was opposition to the euthanasia program from the public and the churches, and it was ended officially in 1941, after two years. Even so, the killings continued and an estimated total of 250,000 mentally and physically disabled people were murdered between 1939 and 1945.

The Genocide of the Roma

When they came into power the Nazis intensified longstanding policies of persecution against the Roma in Germany. The Roma are thought to have come from India and to have arrived in Europe around 1300. They were the only other group besides the Jews who were singled out for annihilation on the grounds of "race."

Like the Jews and people of African descent, the Roma were prohibited from marrying Germans under the September 1935 laws for the "Protection of German Blood and Honor." In 1937, they were deprived of their civil rights, along with Jews. And as they did with Jews, the government encouraged brutality against the Roma. During a so-called Gypsy Clean-up Week in 1938, Roma in Austria and Germany were rounded up, beaten and sent to prison. They were ghettoized in special camps outside cities that were guarded by the SS (*Schutzstaffel*, or Protective Squadrons, a special guard of soldiers and policemen that was somewhat independent so its activities could not be attributed to the government or to the Nazi Party). In December 1938, a document by Henrich Himmler, leader of the SS and the Gestapo (the political arm of the police), referred to "The Final Solution to the Gypsy Question."

Roma from Germany and countries under the Nazi occupation were then rounded up and sent to the work and death camps. Five thousand Austrian Roma were killed in mobile gas vans in Chelmno, Poland, in December 1941. In 1942, Himmler decreed that Roma were to be sent to Auschwitz. There, they were forced to wear black triangles to identify them.

Like the Jews, many Roma were used in medical experiments, particularly the infamous Dr. Josef Mengele's study of twins, before being killed.[10] Roma were forced to build a new camp, at Auschwitz, Birkenau, where about 20,000 of them eventually died.

The Roma genocide was overlooked after the war, and it was many years before the story was told. An estimated 500,000 Roma people were killed during the Holocaust.

Other Targets of Persecution

Poles and Russians and other Slavs were savagely targeted by the Nazis. Three million Christian Poles were killed and 3.3 million Soviet prisoners in German concentration camps died in captivity. About 25 million Soviets died during the German invasion of the USSR.

Leftists, Afro-Germans, gay men and Jehovah's Witnesses were also persecuted. They were not gassed, but many were killed or died in terrible conditions in the camps.

Jehovah's Witnesses refused to pledge their loyalty to the Nazis. They were deemed "dangerous" traitors and sent to prison.

The few people of African origin in Germany in the early 1930s were discriminated against even before Hitler came to power. But they then became targeted along with many others. About 500 Afro-German teenagers were sterilized. Others were used in medical experiments. Some German and other European and American blacks were sent to concentration camps and died there. The number who died or were killed is unknown.

In 1935, the Nazis established an Office for Combating Homosexuality and Abortion. (The link between homosexuality and abortion indicates Nazi distress over the falling birth rate and the concern that gay men would not be fathering children.) In Germany, informers of all kinds, including school children, were encouraged to "out" gay men, who were then arrested and sent to concentration camps. Lesbians were not generally targeted.

Gay men were forced to wear pink triangles to identify them in the concentration camps. They were more harshly treated than "ordinary" criminals or political prisoners and were the first to be used for medical experiments, which few survived. Gay men were often castrated or tortured or terrorized in other ways in the camps. They were also "re-educated." Estimates of the numbers of gay men killed range from 10,000 to 15,000.

Chapter 5
The Anatomy of a Genocide

> First they came for the Communists, but I was not a Communist — so I said nothing. Then they came for the Social Democrats, but I was not a Social Democrat — so I did nothing. Then came the trade unionists, but I was not a trade unionist. And then they came for the Jews, but I was not a Jew — so I did little. Then when they came for me, there was no one left who could stand up for me.
>
> — Martin Niemoeller[1]

Who Are the Victims?

As this famous quote illustrates, there are often several categories of victims in a genocide. One set of victims may be chosen because they are a hated group that appears to be a threat to the perpetrators (e.g., the Armenians, the Jews, the Tutsis) and another because they may oppose the genocide (e.g., communists, moderate Hutus). The victims are usually vulnerable people in a society because they are hated or feared, because they are an elite minority, because they lack power.

The first victims are often the most prominent people in the community — its political and religious leaders, intellectuals and teachers. These are the people most likely to have the ability to organize some resistance to the perpetrators, so they are usually the first people targeted. And the majority of those first targeted are usually men.

Isolating the Victims

A great deal of planning and organization is necessary to carry out a genocide. Often the first step is taking away the rights of the people in the targeted group, steadily excluding them from society by making it impossible for them to go to school or marry or make a living. In Nazi Germany, for example, early steps in the genocidal process involved taking away Jewish people's right to own businesses, and mentally and physically disabled people's right to have children.

The planners manage to take away people's rights by reinforcing an "us-them" situation built on old conflicts, racism or ethnocentrism and making it seem "natural" or "right" that the target group is brutally discriminated against. Soon people in the group are not just criticized and humiliated but dehumanized. The underlying logic is that if people in the targeted group are not human, then they can be killed without remorse.

The separating out of the target group or groups is often followed by their actual physical isolation. In German-occupied Poland, Jewish people were moved into a ghetto, where they were essentially under siege. The Hereros and the Armenians were both forced to flee

Words Can Kill

A recognizable type of hate language is used in genocide. People are described as animals, as pigs or rats or cockroaches, which many humans are more able to imagine killing than other humans. They may be described as sub-human, as savages, as the native peoples were, or as thieves and criminals, as the Roma were depicted. Or they may be "godless" or, as in the Soviet Union, "enemies of the people" or " parasites who had no soul," as the kulaks were described. In every case, people are dehumanized in order to justify treating them badly and even killing them.

The flip side of hate language is euphemism — that is, substituting a mild, vague or less "embarrassing" word or phrase for the explicit, direct word or words. It is commonly used in genocide to cover up the killing. The Gulf War in 1990-91, for example, (though not a genocide) popularized the use of "collateral damage" to mean dead civilians. In Nazi Germany, the "euthanasia" program had nothing to do with mercy killing. It was the outright murder of disabled people. During the Rwanda genocide, "going to work" meant going to kill Tutsis. In Bosnia-Herzegovina, "population resettlement" was a euphemism for getting rid of Muslims.

Extreme sexist language, and the denigration of women as whores, sluts and slaves, joins racist and dehumanizing language and euphemism to facilitate and justify a genocide.[2]

their homes. A forced march ending in a massacre or starvation was also a characteristic of the Cambodian genocide. And the people of Darfur have been driven out of their homes and compelled to seek shelter in crowded refugee camps that they cannot leave for fear of being raped or killed.

The perpetrators of a genocide often use the media to spread messages of hate and dis-information about the group they want to victimize. A talk radio station, Radio Milles Collines, set up less than a year before the April 1994 Rwandan genocide, referred to Tutsis as cockroaches, spoke of a Tutsi conspiracy to seize power and played music whose lyrics encouraged Hutus to kill Tutsis. During the genocide itself, broadcasters announced the hiding places of prominent Tutsis. Books, newspapers and especially films were widely used by Nazi Germany to spread hatred against Jews, Roma and the disabled.

Placing people in concentration camps — which were first used by the British in the Boer War in South Africa, from 1899 to 1902 — makes them powerless, at the whim of the guards, never knowing when they will be killed.

Who Are the Perpetrators?

The perpetrators are those who design and carry out and recruit others to carry out the killing. They may feel threatened by the power of the people they are targeting,

Eight Stages of Genocide

Gregory Stanton of Genocide Watch categorizes genocide as a process that develops in eight stages:

1. Classification: People are separated into "us and them."
2. Symbolization: Names or symbols (such as the yellow star for Jews or the black triangle for Roma) are given to the classifications.
3. Dehumanization: The "other group" is equated with "animals, vermin, insects or diseases."
4. Organization: Special army units or militias are trained; the killings are planned.
5. Polarization: Groups are driven apart by extremists; intermarriage or social interaction between groups is forbidden.
6. Preparation: Targeted people are physically separated from others, forced to leave their homes or live in ghettos or concentration camps.
7. Extermination: Mass killing of the group begins.
8. Denial: The perpetrators cover up the evidence of the crimes, deny the crimes and block investigations into the crimes. They stay in power until they are removed by force.

Stanton notes that "the later stages must be preceded by the earlier stages," but that the early stages continue to operate throughout the whole genocidal process. Most important, the genocide can be stopped at each stage, because although the stages are predictable, they are not "inexorable" (i.e., impossible to stop or prevent).[3]

they may have political or economic reasons for wanting to get rid of a group, or they may once have been victims themselves and want revenge.

Perpetrators could be any or all of: a government, an elite group running a government, an army, mercenaries, a militia (or armed group of citizens), government bureaucrats, or "ordinary" citizens. Genocide is not one murder or a few murders, so perpetrators must always enlist others to help them to wipe out a group.

Most genocide is committed by government armies, but private or corporate armies of mercenaries are often hired or brought in to assist with the killing. These "paramilitaries" are experienced, well-armed and more highly motivated than regular soldiers. They're also more used to killing. Significantly, it is easier for governments to deny their involvement in genocidal activities if the atrocities are carried out by paramilitaries.

The janjaweed in Darfur are an example of a group armed and mobilized to help carry out a genocide. Private militias were also used by the Serbs in the former Yugoslavia and by Indonesia in East Timor.

Besides the perpetrators who directly kill during a genocide, there are often others who are involved more indirectly. For example, in Nazi Germany, the work of organizing the transport of Jews and other victims to the labor and death camps was done by thousands of civil servants and business people. These people were often only responsible for one small part of the program, and did not necessarily understand or want to understand all the implications of what they were doing. They were involved, nonetheless.

Getting People to Kill

The first question many people ask about genocide is, how is it possible for human beings to kill other human beings so easily? Most people have a moral and physical repugnance to killing. Even soldiers, who are trained to kill in combat, are often unwilling to kill other soldiers. For example, a study of American riflemen in World War II found that "on average only 15 percent of trained combat riflemen fired their weapons at all in battle."[4] As a result, American army training was transformed to ensure that soldiers shoot unerringly and without thinking. It also stressed that fighting was about protecting one's "buddies" from enemy attack.

Most soldiers and others who have killed many times admit that although the first killing is difficult, it gets easier each time they do it. Some people describe the intoxication that they experience as part of a group killing.

But how do instigators of genocide get ordinary people to overcome their respect for human life? In many cases, it is through people's fear of being killed themselves. Even if most of the killing is taking place outside the public eye, people become aware of the horror of torture and killing. They get the message that the perpetrators are all-powerful and capable of taking lives at any moment. When the events are staged in daylight and in public, as they often were in Rwanda, it also implies that they are lawful and acceptable, making it harder to take a stand against the genocide. The "kill or be killed" situation, in which perpetrators recruit others to help them and threaten them with death if they refuse to participate, is a common element in genocides.

There is also the need to go along with the crowd, to conform to one's group or to support one's country, to be patriotic. And another element is people's obedience to authority, to someone who orders them or encourages them to torture and kill others.

In the 1960s psychologist Stanley Milgram did a series of experiments in which people were instructed to administer electric shocks of increasing severity to supposed "victims" who pleaded with them to stop. He found that most people do what they are told to do, even if it hurts other people, as long as the order to do it comes from someone they see as "a legitimate authority." Milgram argued that only a small percentage of people were able to resist the authority's instructions. Few found it easy to disobey.[5] (Other psychologists have critiqued the inhumane nature of his research and say the question of obedience is more complex than Milgram has presented it, but most agree that at the very least it demonstrates the difficulty many people have in resisting authority.) As a Rwandan *genocidaire* (French for genocidal killer) told French journalist Jean Hatzfeld:

Killing is very discouraging if you yourself must decide to do it, even to an animal. But if you must obey the orders of the authorities, if you have been properly prepared, if you feel yourself pushed and pulled, if you see that the killing will be total and without disastrous consequences for yourself, you feel soothed and reassured. You go off to it with no more worry.[6]

Expectation of Impunity

Many genocides would not take place if the perpetrators believed that they would be punished. But there are so many examples from the past where perpetrators have gotten away with genocide that they are quite sure that they will too.

There are undoubted links between genocides on this point. Hitler noted that no one remembered the Armenians; he also remarked on the genocidal treatment of North American Indians, which he knew Americans and Canadians had denied. Nazi literature was found in the home of President Habyarimana of Rwanda just before the 1994 Rwanda genocide.[7] And the Sudanese government knew from the indifference of the UN and Western countries to the Rwandan genocide while it was taking place that it too could get away with the mass murder of Africans in Darfur.

Who Are the Bystanders?

Bystanders are the people or groups of people or even whole countries who see events take place and who do nothing to stop them. As Martin Niemoeller's famous words that begin this chapter demonstrate, bystanders' indifference and their failure to act allow a genocide to continue. And unless the process of genocide is opposed, it continues to widen and take in more and more groups of victims.

Why don't bystanders act? It may be because of fear of authorities, and fear of being killed themselves. But many people "stand by" watching (or hiding their eyes) even when they are not personally in danger. They may not involve themselves because the "us-them" propaganda has been successful, and therefore they do not identify with the victims or recognize their humanity. (The closer or more related a bystander feels to a victim, the more likely he or she is to act to help.)[8] Maybe the bystanders see victims the way the perpetrators want them to see them — as animals or criminals. At times of crisis, bystanders may believe that getting rid of these people will solve the country's or their own personal problems. In many situations, bystanders have something to gain from the victims' deaths, such as land, money, jobs or consumer goods.

It is impossible to be a neutral bystander in most situations. During the Rwandan genocide, Hutus who refused to kill Tutsis, including their Tutsi wives and

THE CAMBODIAN GENOCIDE

The southeast Asian country of Cambodia became independent from France in 1954. In 1961, an armed resistance movement headed by communist Pol Pot started waging a guerrilla war against Cambodia's leader, Prince Norodom Sihanouk. Pol Pot, which means "Original Cambodian," was the alias used by Saloth Sar, a student from an elite family who studied in Paris and returned to Cambodia in 1953. (His new name not only disguised his connections to Cambodian royalty, but indicated his intense racism against those who were not "pure" Cambodians.)

During the latter part of the Vietnam War, Cambodia, a close neighbor of Vietnam, became the unlucky setting for much of the ground and air war between the United States and Vietnam. One hundred and fifty thousand Cambodian peasants were killed by American bombs between 1969 and 1973. Others fled the dangerous countryside and settled in the capital city, Phnom Penh. These upheavals and US support to a military coup that ousted Prince Sihanouk served to strengthen people's support for Pol Pot.

In 1975, following the withdrawal of American troops from Vietnam and the end of the Vietnam War, the US stopped supporting the Cambodian military government. On April 17, 1975, Pol Pot and his Khmer Rouge army, most of whom were teenaged peasant boys, marched into Phnom Penh and took control of the country, renaming it Democratic Kampuchea (DK).

Pol Pot announced the need to "purify" Cambodian society and declared "This is Year Zero." In a bizarre and brutal attempt to turn back the clock, the country was shut off from all foreign influences, including foreigners themselves, newspapers, radio, television, mail and even money, for the first time in human history. Human rights of any kind were non-existent. There was no free speech. Religion was forbidden in a country where 90 percent of the people were Buddhists. People were not allowed to travel. The whole society was reorganized according to a system of schedules and rules. People were killed for the slightest violation of the smallest rule.

The Khmer Rouge forced inhabitants to leave the cities. Two million people were marched out of Phnom Penh alone. An estimated 20,000 died on the journey. Some, who admitted to being government officials or army officers, were executed. Others died of starvation. Those who made it to the countryside after walking for up to six weeks were forced into slave labor in rice fields and on other agricultural projects. They began to die in the thousands from starvation, overwork and disease. They were told that "whether you live or die is of no great significance."

The Khmer Rouge rounded up and killed former government officials, army officers and soldiers, the educated and the well-off such as doctors, teachers and lawyers, as well as their peasant relatives, and Buddhist monks. Ethnic groups or those who were not "pure Khmer people," including Vietnamese, Chinese, Thai and Muslims, were also genocide victims. Early on, 150,000 Vietnamese Cambodians were deported and the 10,000 who were left were murdered in 1977 and 1978. By 1979, 100,000 Cham Muslims of a total population of 250,000 in the east of the country had been killed or starved or worked to death. Only 2,000 of the country's 70,000 Buddhist monks survived.

Many different political, social and ethnic groups in Cambodia were targeted by the Khmer Rouge — all those who opposed the regime or were even suspected of opposing it. A series of perceived threats in different parts of the country led to increased arrests and massacres and, finally, a mutiny by some of the Khmer Rouge forces. These rebels crossed the border and asked for help from the Vietnamese. Vietnam invaded Cambodia on December 25, 1978. The Vietnamese took Phnom Penh on January 7, 1979, and Pol Pot sought exile in Thailand.

The genocide was over. The Vietnamese withdrew in 1989 and the country was renamed Cambodia. Pol Pot lived in Thailand for almost twenty years and news accounts indicate that he died in his sleep in April 1998.

A total of 1.7 million Cambodians were killed during the genocide out of a population of 7.1 million.

Tuol Sleng Prison

The largest of many prisons in the country during the Cambodian genocide was Security Office 21 or S21. It is now the site of the Tuol Sleng Genocide Museum.

A former high school, S21 was a death center for political prisoners. The classrooms were divided into a torture unit and an interrogation unit. Thousands of tortured prisoners were forced to confess, "I am not a human being; I am an animal" before they were murdered. We know this because, amazingly, many of these confessions were recorded. The Khmer Rouge also photographed and recorded the vital statistics of 6,000 of the prisoners (including whole families of "traitors") before they were killed. These photographs — of children, women and men, of mothers and babies — survive to remind us of the horror of S21.

Only seven people of a total 17,000 to 20,000 survived their detention at S21. One was Vann Nath, a man who was singled out because he was an artist. One day guards removed his shackles and handed him a paintbrush. He began painting pictures of Pol Pot, a man he had never seen. "Every brush stroke," he told a journalist in 2002, "you were just hoping that they would like it and would let you live."[9]

Mr Vann Nath managed to escape in the tumult of the Vietnamese invasion in January 1979. But he still hears the screams of the victims. He told the journalist, "I want to forget. I try to forget, but it is useless. I can't forget even a small part of it. Even after [more than] 20 years, when I think of it, I can still feel terrified."

husbands, were themselves targeted. There were only two possibilities: to go along with the perpetrators or to resist and risk being killed yourself. This should act as a reminder to bystanders who are outside a situation — like most of us in relation to Darfur — and who are capable of responding without threatening their own lives, that they *must* respond.

Genocide and Gender

Genocide refers to the intention to wipe out a particular group of people — men, women and children. So how do issues of gender relate to genocide? In fact, perpetrators often make clear distinctions between men and women, between boys and girls during a genocide.

Men are usually the first to be killed, because in most cultures men still predominate as leaders and hold the key positions in a society. They are the people the perpetrators want to get rid of immediately in order to consolidate their power. Perpetrators also expect men to be more of a physical threat than women (or young children), and they want to isolate and kill them before they organize to resist the genocide.

Men were targeted first during the Armenian genocide. It was also the pattern in East Timor when the Indonesians invaded in 1975. There, women, small children and elderly men were set aside from the boys and men, who were then machine-gunned on the spot. It happened in Bosnia from 1992 to 1995 and in Kosovo in 1999, where Serbian forces in the former Yugoslavia separated out Bosnian and Albanian men as the first victims of torture and killing.

In most genocides, men are more likely to do the killing. However, women have been shown to be just as brutal killers as men in certain situations, including Nazi Germany, Cambodia and Rwanda.[10] Women may appear to be protected in some genocidal situations, but in most cases they are just not killed off as quickly. Even that is not always true. For example, pregnant women and women with young children entering Auschwitz and some other Nazi concentration camps were the first to be gassed, along with their children. Single women and men, as long as they were healthy enough to work, sometimes survived a little longer.

However, women as a group are victimized during a genocide through extreme sexual violence and rape.

Rape and Sexual Violence
Rape and other types of sexual violence have been committed against women and girls for thousands of years. Rape is often considered to be an isolated act of brutality, and because it is related to sex, it is repressed (and therefore denied) or ignored. But rape is also used as a military, even a genocidal weapon. During a genocide it is an act of violence that is almost always committed together with other brutal acts — kidnapping, beating, torture and murder. Amnesty International's Irene Kahn explains:

Custom, culture and religion have built an image of women as bearing the "honor" of their communities. Disparaging a woman's sexuality and destroying her physical integrity have become a means by which to terrorize, demean and "defeat" entire communities, as well as to punish, intimidate and humiliate women.[11]

Native American scholar Andrea Smith sees sexual violence as central to the colonization of Native Americans and the genocidal destruction of their culture. She maintains that this genocidal relationship continues, making aboriginal women more "rapable" than other women and their rape and killing less carefully prosecuted than that of other North American women.[12] In Canada, for example, according to Amnesty International, young indigenous women are five times more likely to die from violence than other women.[13] This violence usually begins with sexual violence.

Rape can also be a way of controlling or blocking a woman's ability to bear children — one way of contributing to the destruction or extermination of a national, ethnic, racial or religious group. Ten years after the Bosnian genocide, two women journalists found that victims of rape were stigmatized and unable to claim the war-victim status that would provide them with needed employment assistance and health benefits. Very few of the women were living with the children of the rapes.

GENOCIDE IN BOSNIA-HERZEGOVINA

The break-up of the Soviet bloc took a violent form in the dissolution of Yugoslavia, which began to divide up along ethnic and religious lines in the early 1990s. In 1992 in Bosnia-Herzegovina, the Bosnian Serbs declared a state linked to the ethnically "pure" Greater Serbia under the leadership of Radovan Karadzic. They began the brutal persecution of Bosnian Muslims (or Bosniaks). Muslims were forced to leave their towns and villages in the northern and eastern parts of the country. This practice, termed "ethnic cleansing," was a prelude to genocide.

Muslim men were sent to concentration camps, tortured and murdered. The worst massacre of the genocide took place during six days at Srebrenica from July 11 to 16, 1995. There, under the eyes of international peacekeepers, the Serbian forces separated the city's men (all those between the ages of 11 and 65) from the women. The men and boys were loaded onto trucks or buses and driven to execution sites in isolated locations where they were shot — 8,000 of them.

During the genocide, an estimated 50,000 Muslim women were captured and taken to schools or community centers where they were gang-raped and continually abused, for days or weeks or months at a time. The rapists told the women that they wanted to impregnate them so that they would have Serb babies. Once pregnant, the women were often kept imprisoned until it was too late for them to have safe abortions.

An estimated 200,000 of a total population of 3.2 million Bosnian Muslims were killed in Bosnia-Herzegovina.

Many had abandoned them to orphanages, and in a few cases, the women had murdered their children.[14]

In the era of HIV/AIDS, rape carries a death sentence even for women who manage to survive the sexual violence. A 1999 study by Avega-Agahozo, a Rwandan widows' organization, showed that two-thirds of the 250,000 to 500,000 women victims of rape and sexual violence during the 1994 genocide were HIV positive. By 2004, only 2,000 Rwandan men and women were receiving lifesaving anti-retroviral drugs.

Rape Recognized as a Genocidal Act

Many survivors of rape do not want to talk about their experiences for fear of being blamed or rejected by their families or communities. It is only through tireless support from feminists and intensive advocacy by feminist and human rights organizations that rape and sexual violence have finally been recognized as crimes under international law.

The International Criminal Tribunal for Rwanda was the first to define rape as a genocidal act. On September 2, 1998, the Rwanda Tribunal found the former mayor of Taba in central Rwanda, Jean-Paul Akayesu, guilty of genocide, crimes against humanity and war crimes. The Akayesu Judgment defined rape as an act of aggression similar to torture, and "one of the worst ways of inflicting harm on the victim as he or she suffers both bodily and mental harm." The judgment makes clear that although men and boys are also victims of rape and sexual violence, it is women and girls who are targeted in most cases.

In February 2001, three Bosnian Serb soldiers at the International Criminal Tribunal for the Former Yugoslavia were found guilty of mass rape and sexual enslavement, which were recognized as crimes against humanity.

The new International Criminal Court (ICC), building on the experience of these two tribunals, has developed a detailed and expansive definition of sexual violence under the heading of crimes against humanity and war crimes.

Comfort Women

During the Second World War, thousands of teenaged women were sexually enslaved and sent to war zones to "service" the imperial Japanese forces. Most of the "comfort women" were Korean, but women from other occupied countries, including Taiwan, Indonesia, Burma and the Philippines, were also forced into sexual slavery. The women were held in "comfort stations" where they were brutally gang-raped, beaten, mutilated and sometimes murdered. It is estimated that just a third of the 200,000 comfort women were still alive at the end of the war. Only in 1993, after pressure by organizations of survivors with support from feminists, did the Japanese government admit its official involvement in the recruitment of the comfort women.

Chapter 6
Responding to Genocide

> We will recommend to our government not to
> intervene as the risks are high and all that is here
> are humans.
>> — Western bureaucrats to General Romeo
>> Dallaire in Rwanda, April 1994[1]

The events of World War II, especially the Holocaust,
gave rise to a series of international efforts to try to
ensure that human rights were respected and that genocide would never take place again. But the Universal
Declaration and the Genocide Convention may as well
have been ghost documents written in disappearing ink
for all the protection they provided for the half century
following the war.

The Genocide Convention had foreseen the development of an international criminal court that would be
capable of prosecuting people who were suspected of
committing genocide. This did not come into being for
over fifty years.

A few isolated attempts to use the Genocide Convention were sidelined and, in the case of an African American petition to the UN in 1951, the activists were harassed and persecuted. Some positive changes in human rights worldwide were evident in the 1960s, with widespread opposition to the war in Vietnam and to South African apartheid. In 1967, the UN described apartheid as a "crime against humanity" and called for economic sanctions against South Africa. But these were the exceptions.

"We Charge Genocide"

African American singer Paul Robeson and William L. Patterson, a lawyer and executive director of the Civil Rights Congress, presented petitions signed by eminent African Americans to the UN in December 1951 in both New York and Paris.

Called "We Charge Genocide: the Crime of Government Against the Negro People," the petition focused on the killing of at least 10,000 African Americans in the US since the abolition of slavery in 1865. It provided a "record of mass slayings on the basis of race" and "the willful creation of conditions making for premature death, poverty and disease." It reminded the UN that genocide does not just refer to physical extermination but to "any intent to destroy, in whole or in part, a national, racial, or religious group."[2]

US officials made sure that the petition was ignored

by the UN — copies of the petition sent to London and Paris mysteriously never arrived. Robeson and Patterson were branded as traitors and spies for the Soviet Union and persecuted for years afterwards. Although the merits of the case have never had a formal hearing, the petition stands out as a courageous first step in the launching of the civil rights movement, which demanded equality for African Americans in the US.

A People's Tribunal

An International War Crimes Tribunal set up in 1966 by writers and philosophers Bertrand Russell and Jean-Paul Sartre found the United States guilty of genocide in Vietnam. The tribunal argued that the entire Vietnamese population was threatened with extermination by massive bombings, often with weapons that were forbidden by the laws of war (e.g., Agent Orange, a weed-killer containing toxic chemicals like the known carcinogen, dioxin).

Sartre described the situation as "the greatest power on earth against a poor peasant people," adding that "genocide presents itself as the *only possible reaction* to the rising of a whole people against its oppressors."[3] Sartre also accused the US of trying to intimidate the rest of the world by demonstrating what would happen to anyone who dared to fight them.

Legally speaking, although American aggression against the Vietnamese people was undoubtedly a serious human rights crime, it was not strictly speaking genocide. It apparently comes under the war crime of aggression, which has yet to be defined by the International Criminal Court.[4]

The "people's tribunal," as it was commonly called, has not been forgotten. In 2003, it provided the model for the World Tribunal on Iraq, a global initiative that grew out of widespread opposition to the war in Iraq (which like the Vietnam War, would qualify as a war crime of aggression).[5]

Avoiding the "G" Word

Why, following the post-war promises, were international human rights so systematically ignored? And why was the Genocide Convention of such little practical use for so long?

There are many reasons. A major factor was the Cold War, a standoff of ruthless rivalry, including a competition in the build-up of nuclear arms, between the United States and the Soviet Union and their respective allies. It raged from 1947 to 1991 and made it almost impossible for the countries lined up on one side or the other to agree on human rights issues at the United Nations. Another factor was that the Human Rights Commission set up by the UN in 1947 to promote human rights did not take up the many complaints of human rights violations it received, focusing instead on defining rights and drafting international agreements and reports. It finally began to address violations in the 1960s, in particular the problem of apartheid in South Africa.

Another element was governments' and the UN's fear that if a situation was called a genocide, then they might be called upon to intervene to stop the atrocities. There was always some reason for not acting. On the one hand, the perpetrators might be important allies or trading partners. On the other, the country where the genocide was taking place might have been of insufficient strategic interest to care about. As a result, perpetrator governments continued to commit gross human rights violations — including genocide — with impunity.

The next worldwide recognition of genocide did not occur until after the end of the Rwandan genocide in 1994. The instances of genocide or "politicide" (a term used by Genocide Watch to refer to the extermination of political groups, because it is not explicitly part of the UN genocide definition) that took place between World War II and 1994 include:

- the massacres of 500,000 Indonesian leftists by the Indonesian government in 1965-66;
- the killing of 3 million Bangladeshis and the rape of 250,000 girls and women by Pakistan during the 1971 Bangladesh liberation war;
- the killing of 200,000 to 300,000 Hutus by the mainly Tutsi army in Burundi from May to July 1972;
- the killing of 200,000 people in East Timor by

Indonesia, beginning in 1975 and continuing until UN peacekeepers arrived in 1999;

- the genocide of 1.7 million Cambodians by the Khmer Rouge from 1975-79;
- the killing of more than 200,000, mainly Mayans, by the government in Guatemala from 1981-83;
- the killing of an estimated 182,000 Kurds by Iraq in 1988;
- the killing of 200,000 Bosnians by the Serbs in Bosnia-Herzegovina in the former Yugoslavia from 1992-95.

Genocide has still not been acknowledged in many of these countries, by the perpetrators themselves or by other governments that stood by and let it happen. In many cases, the killings have been swept under the carpet of history.

New Rights Initiatives

A number of other international human rights conventions and treaties did finally follow the Universal Declaration of Human Rights and the Genocide Convention (see timeline, page 117).[6] And in the early 1990s, with the end of the Cold War, individuals and governments turned more and more to the information collected by human rights groups like Amnesty International and Human Rights Watch and United

Nations agencies to make decisions about situations of conflict that had the potential of becoming genocidal.

Proposals presented to the UN to set up a court to try the leaders of the Khmer Rouge for genocide and crimes against humanity in Cambodia failed in the 1990s, finally succeeding only in 2004 (with the first trials slated to begin in 2007). But persistent media attention to the situation in the former Yugoslavia, and perhaps the realization that genocide (or at least "ethnic cleansing," a less weighty term) was once more taking place in "civilized" Europe, brought the Yugoslav Tribunal into being.

The Yugoslav Tribunal

The International Criminal Tribunal for the Former Yugoslavia was set up in May 1993 to prosecute those responsible for crimes against humanity since 1991. The tribunal has focused on bringing those who ordered the crimes — the senior political and military leadership — to trial. Former Serbian president Slobodan Milosevic was charged on sixty-six counts of genocide, crimes against humanity and war crimes. Milosevic escaped justice, however. He died in March 2006, just months before the expected end of his four-year-long trial.

The first Yugoslav trial did not start until 1996, and many criminals who should have been detained are still at large (most notably former Bosnian Serb president Radovan Karadzic). Yet the court has produced a crucial history of the chain of events in the former Yugoslavia and has developed valuable legal opinions and precedents. The tribunal's operations are broadcast on the Internet at www.un.org/icty/.

The Rwanda Tribunal

The first major recognition of the Genocide Convention came with the establishment of the International Criminal Tribunal for Rwanda in November 1994. The court was given the mandate to deal with charges of genocide and other violations of international humanitarian law that had taken place during the Rwandan genocide.

Based in Arusha, Tanzania, which borders on Rwanda, the Rwanda Tribunal has completed the trials of twenty-five defendants. The majority of them are high-level political and military officials and civil servants of the former Hutu-controlled government, including the main organizer of the genocide, Théoneste Bagosora; former prime minister Jean Kambanda; the director of the Milles Collines radio station; and militia leaders. On September 4, 1998, Mr Kambanda, who had pleaded guilty to genocide, was the highest-level official ever to be convicted by an international tribunal. He was given the maximum sentence — life imprisonment.

The judgment from the trial of Jean-Paul Akayesu (see Rape Recognized as a Genocidal Act, page 74) was a landmark in two ways. Not only was it the first time rape had been found to be an act of genocide,

THE RWANDAN GENOCIDE

In 1994, Rwanda was a country of about 8 million people, 14 percent Tutsi and 85 percent Hutu. The other 1 percent of the population was Twa (or Batwa), one of the Pygmy groups indigenous to central and western Africa. Traditionally, the Hutus were peasant farmers and the Tutsis were cattle owners and the elite. It is unclear exactly how this division of labor arose. What is clear is that the harsh Belgian colonial rule, starting in 1918, worsened the situation.

The Belgians reinforced the idea, largely introduced by Roman Catholic missionaries, that the Hutus were native to Rwanda, and the Tutsis were a superior, more "civilized" people from the north. In the 1930s the Belgians introduced identity cards that indicated ethnicity. Even so, the Hutus and Tutsis continued to speak the same language, Kinyarwanda (as well as the French of the colonialists), and to intermarry. In their shared language, however, Hutu means "servant" and Tutsi means "rich in cattle." The stereotype was that Hutus were short and stocky and Tutsis were tall and thin, although both Hutus and Tutsis say that it is often impossible to tell them apart. (Otherwise, why would they need identity cards?)

There is a long pre-history to the 1994 genocide, and many power changes in both Rwanda and Burundi (a neighboring country that like Rwanda is densely populated, mainly by Tutsis and Hutus). There were at least five previous mass killings, beginning with the Hutu revolution in 1959, which changed the country's leaders from Tutsi to Hutu.

About 1 million Tutsis who had fled Rwanda during these massacres lived in refugee camps in Uganda. Eventually, the exiles built up an army called the Rwandan Patriotic Front (RPF). The RPF invaded Rwanda in 1990 but were held off when the Rwandan government troops were helped by French paratroopers.

Inside Rwanda, the government of President Juvenal Habyarimana encouraged violence against the Tutsis and began giving military training to militias of young men who later became the Interahamwe ("those who stand together"). Radio Mille Collines and the twice-monthly newspaper *Kangura*, along with other media, broadcast anti-Tutsi propaganda. Divisions between the Hutus and Tutsis widened.

Under pressure from Western governments beginning in 1992, the government agreed to peace talks. The Arusha Peace Agreement signed in Tanzania on August 4, 1993, mandated power sharing between Tutsis and Hutus, but the government appeared unprepared to go along with this. Canadian general Romeo Dallaire was appointed to lead the peace-keeping team to oversee the accord. He arrived in Kigali in October 1993, commanding an initial force of 1,200 UN blue beret troops.

The government had been building up caches of assault rifles, guns and grenades as well as farm implements such as machetes and axes. (The arms were supplied mainly by France, which continued to train troops and advise the government on political and military matters until the genocide began, and Egypt.) Militia members were being trained to use explosives and weapons and to kill people quick-ly. The names and addresses of Tutsis were prepared in advance. Children, who did not have identity cards, had already been separat-ed in schools, Tutsis on one side, Hutus on the other.

General Dallaire learned of the arms build-up in January 1994, four months before the genocide started, from an Interahamwe informant — a Hutu who opposed the RPF, but was horrified by the government's carefully organized death-squad plans to kill 1,000 people in twenty minutes. The informant said the government planned to kill ten Belgian peacekeepers and assumed that the peacekeeping mission would cave in if the Belgians left. Yet when Dallaire relayed the information and stated his intention to seize the weapons to his UN bosses in New York, he was ordered to stop. Every attempt Dallaire made to oppose the coming genocide was thwarted by the UN, so that by the time the genocide began, there was little the small peacekeeping force could do to protect people.

The spark that kindled the genocide was the shooting down of the presidential plane on April 6, 1994. The crash killed both Rwandan president Habyarimana and the president of Burundi, Cyprien Ntaryamira. It is still not clear who manned the surface-to-air missiles — the president's associates, who then used it as an excuse to start the genocide, or the RPF. In any case, only a few hours after the crash, the presidential guard, government troops and militia killed moderate Hutu officials and opposition leaders — anyone likely to oppose the genocide — and began the systematic extermination of Tutsis countrywide. The ringleader of the genocide appears to have been a top defense ministry official named Colonel Théoneste Bagosora.

The next day, Prime Minister Agathe Uwilingiyimana and her husband were murdered. So were the ten Belgian peacekeepers who had been guarding them, causing the Belgian government to pull out its remaining peacekeepers, just as the genocidaires had planned. Well-equipped French, Belgian and Italian soldiers arrived and quickly evacuated their own and other Western nationals. They failed to join the United Nations Assistance Mission for Rwanda (UNAMIR), leaving Dallaire's meager force alone to face the genocide — and leaving the Rwandan Tutsis and moderate Hutus to their fate.

Once the killing began, the troops and the Interahamwe encouraged or forced other Hutus to take part, even to kill members of their own families. Although some Hutus sheltered their Tutsi relatives, friends and neighbors, hundreds of thousands joined in the slaughter. Many of the Interahamwe and other militia were unemployed youths, but they were joined by people from all sectors of society, including teachers, journalists, priests, ministers and doctors.

The killing took place openly, everywhere — in people's houses, on the street, at roadblocks, in public stadiums, even in churches, hospitals and schools, where groups of Tutsis had gathered for safety. Some of the worst massacres took place in churches, where church officials often joined in the massacres themselves. In Musha, 40 kilometers (24 miles) north of the capital, Kigali, 1,200 people were killed in a church in a single day. The method of killing people sheltered inside buildings was to first toss in grenades and then shoot or hack people to death as they ran out.

The militia had learned in their training that cutting the Achilles tendons on the back of people's heels would make it impossible for them to run, so the genocidaires could return and kill them later.

Tutsi women suffered vicious rape and torture before they were killed. Some, half-dead from starvation and beatings and constant rape, were kept as sex slaves for weeks or months. Thirty-five-year-old Athanasie Mukarwego's husband was tortured to death on April 14 in Kigali. The Hutu militia told her, "You, we will kill with rape. Did you know that it kills too?" Miraculously, Ms Mukarwego survived and she did not contract HIV/AIDS. But ten years after the genocide she was still living constantly with its horror.[7]

Reports of the mass killings were sent out from Rwanda by the RPF, the Red Cross and many other organizations as the genocide progressed. But instead of strengthening its forces, the UN, led by an aggressive US campaign, pulled out troops, leaving a tiny force of about 400. The UN later reversed this decision due to extreme pressure as the genocide continued. But no reinforcements ever reached Dallaire until after the genocide ended.

Why was the world so willing to look the other way? There are a number of reasons. The US had just six months earlier lost eighteen troops in Somalia. The Western world's focus was on "ethnic cleansing" in the former Yugoslavia. In May 1994, at the height of the genocide, 2,500 journalists were in South Africa to mark the inauguration of Nelson Mandela as president. Few ventured to Rwanda to check out the situation there.[8]

The most important reason is also the hardest to stomach: aside from France, which was still supporting the Hutu regime, Western countries had nothing to gain from preventing the genocide. Rwanda was a poor, mainly agricultural African country. It offered no oil, minerals or other resources valued by the West. As the quotation at the beginning of the chapter states, "All that is here are humans." General Dallaire wonders, throughout his book, "Are we all human, or are some more human than others?"[9]

The RPF finally managed to defeat the Hutu troops and militia in July 1994, and the genocide came to an end. An estimated 800,000 to 1 million people had been murdered. A Tutsi-led government has been in power since.

It was the end of the Rwandan genocide, but the beginning of another catastrophe, as 2 million genocidaires and other Hutus fled to neighboring Zaire (now Democratic Republic of the Congo, DRC). There, the spillover of genocidaires fueled two successive wars. First, Rwandan, Ugandan and anti-Mobutu Congolese cleared out the refugee camps and moved on to overthrow Zairian president Mobutu. Nine African countries were caught up in the second war, which officially ended in 2002, but is still ongoing. In March 2005, the 10,000-strong Interahamwe-based Democratic Forces for the Liberation of Rwanda agreed to stop fighting and return to Rwanda, where President Paul Kagame said they would face trials for involvement in the genocide. It is hoped that their return will help bring peace to the DRC and lower the chances of genocide there. But the situation remains very tense.

September 2, 1998, was also the first time an international court had convicted anyone of genocide under the Genocide Convention.

The International Criminal Court

The accomplishments of the Yugoslav and Rwanda tribunals prepared the way for the establishment of the permanent court envisioned in the Genocide Convention.

The International Criminal Court (ICC) was set up in July 2002 in the Hague, the Netherlands, to prosecute individuals who are responsible for genocide, other crimes against humanity and war crimes. Unlike the International Court of Justice (ICJ), established by the UN in 1945 to settle disputes between countries, the ICC can charge individuals.

The ICC will work with countries' own national courts and provide expertise to nations that want to prosecute criminals themselves. Most important, it will help ensure that people who might not be prosecuted in their own countries can still face charges.

The definition of genocide that the court uses is that of the Genocide Convention. Lemkin's work remains indispensable, but it is disappointing that political and social groups are still not included in the definition.

Building on the experience of the two other tribunals, the ICC includes violent sexual crimes under crimes against humanity and war crimes. It provides a broader definition of these crimes than ever before, covering "rape,

The Gacaca Courts

Following the Rwanda genocide, about 120,000 "ordinary" people alleged to have participated in the killing and sexual violence were imprisoned. The government introduced a community justice system, called gacaca (pronounced "ga-CHA-cha," which means "on the grass"), based in part on traditional conflict resolution, to try these people. The gacaca courts bring accused perpetrators, survivors and witnesses together at the actual scene of the crime to bring out the truth. About 11,000 village tribunals are to be set up, with thousands of judges elected by villagers themselves. This innovative experiment in mass justice and reconciliation is being widely watched around the world.

sexual slavery, enforced prostitution, forced pregnancy, enforced sterilization, or any other form of sexual violence of comparable gravity" (Article 7, Rome Statute).[10]

A number of important countries have not ratified the ICC. International agreements may be signed by governments at their launching, but they must then be ratified, or made legally valid, by the governments or parliaments of their countries. China, India, Indonesia, Pakistan and Turkey never signed the ICC's Rome Statute. Egypt, Iran, Israel, Russia and the US signed but then refused to ratify it. By 2006, 100 of 191 UN member states had ratified the ICC. Countries that do not ratify the treaty cannot make decisions about the ICC or nominate its prosecutor or judges. Of course, they can also make the case that they are not bound by the court's decisions.

The ICC, which can only investigate crimes committed since its inception, is working on cases in four countries, including the Central African Republic, the Democratic Republic of the Congo, Uganda and Sudan (Darfur). To date, the court has issued warrants for the arrest of four leaders of the Lord's Resistance Army in Uganda, but has yet to try anyone.

Impact of the International Courts

The international courts have all been heavily criticized – for plodding along slowly, for being too costly or for being too influenced by politics or by victors' justice. But they have also been praised for finally bringing individuals, however few, to trial for genocide and crimes against humanity, and for their important definitions of sexual violence and rape as genocidal acts or crimes against humanity.

These courts are a clear improvement on the Nuremberg Tribunal, which functioned not as an international court but as a court run by the victors of World War II. Unlike Nuremberg, where twelve defendants convicted of crimes against humanity were hanged, there is no death penalty in the UN tribunals. They follow the principle that even those responsible for serious human rights abuses must be treated humanely.

Memory and Forgetting

French philosopher Jean Baudrillard says that "Forgetting the extermination is part of the extermination itself," reminding us that forgetting a genocide or denying that a genocide took place is built into the perpetrators' planning of the crime.[11] Therefore, part of countering a genocide is ensuring that the events are remembered and talked about, that the history is written down, discussed and passed on.

It is crucial not just to remember those who died, but to understand how and why a genocide happened in order to work against it happening again. And remembering is also necessary to help survivors and the victimized group as a whole begin to recover from their trauma.

Helping the Survivors

Most genocide survivors suffer from some degree of "survivor syndrome" or post-traumatic stress disorder. The symptoms of this trauma have basic features in common with other kinds of trauma, such as those experienced by soldiers and victims of sexual violence.

Psychologist Judith Herman notes that "the ordinary response to atrocities is to banish them from consciousness. Certain violations…are too terrible to utter aloud: this is the meaning of the word *unspeakable*."[12] She points out that victims' symptoms simultaneously call attention to their "unspeakable secret" and try to "deflect attention from it." Victims go back and forth between feeling numb and reliving their terrible experiences. Typical symptoms include great anxiety, sleeplessness, memory problems, depression and withdrawal. What

Herman and many others dealing with survivors of various kinds have learned is that the healing process is a long one. It begins with the victims needing to feel safe. Then they must tell and re-tell their stories to people who listen carefully and with compassion. Finally, they need to be able to re-connect to their communities.

This is not an easy process. Talking about the "unspeakable" is difficult by definition. Most survivors at some level just want to be able to forget what happened to them and to the loved ones they have lost. Many survivors also suffer from guilt that they survived while others were killed. Some never feel safe again. Their depression, anxiety and withdrawal sometimes make it hard for others to relate to them and listen and respond to them in the way that is necessary for their recovery.

The same trauma that affects people at the individual level may affect a society as a whole. So the same process of telling and re-telling the stories is necessary. This is one of the main purposes of the truth and reconciliation commissions that have been set up in many countries.

Apologies and Reparations

Nothing can compensate for the enormous losses sustained during a genocide. But recognition that a crime has occurred is a crucial first step. Apologies, when they are genuine and involve accepting some responsibility for a genocide, can be an important step beyond the acknowledgment that a genocide has taken place. But

Perpetrators' Response

Researchers who have interviewed perpetrators after a genocide have often been struck by their lack of trauma over their involvement in torture and mass killings. Jean Hatzfeld, who interviewed ten Rwandan genocidaires, offers this explanation:

> The absolute character of their project was what allowed them to carry it out with a certain equanimity.... The monstrous nature of the extermination haunts the survivors and even tortures them with guilt, whereas it exculpates and reassures the killers, perhaps protecting them from madness.[13]

Psychologist Ervin Staub suggests that the strength of the Nazi goal offered SS officers similar psychological protection:

> The Nazi goal required the abandonment of ordinary human morality. To accomplish it the goal had to acquire great importance and special intensity. The SS went a long way toward fulfilling it, investing not only enormous effort, time, and resources, but also their identity.[14]

In each case, it is the horrifying totality of the project that both propels the perpetrators to commit genocidal acts and then defends them from remorse.

unless they are sincere and involve some action — some payment or reparation — they may be meaningless. For example, former US president Bill Clinton and UN secretary general Kofi Annan have both apologized to Rwandans for the genocide there, but both also claim that they didn't have enough knowledge to act, which is clearly untrue.[15]

Reparations go beyond apologies to provide financial compensation as well as health and social benefits and public memorials to genocide survivors or victims' relatives or communities. Human rights lawyer Martha Minow points out that the process of seeking reparations itself may be the most important part of the procedure, because it allows survivors a chance to tell their stories.[16]

Germany has paid reparations to Jewish survivors and to the state of Israel in recognition of the Holocaust. There are few other examples of reparations for a genocide, although a number of groups are claiming them. The Hereros have made a claim against the German government and Korean "comfort women" are demanding reparations from the Japanese. The Organization of African Unity's report on the Rwandan genocide also called for reparations from the international community to compensate Rwandan survivors, arguing that "Apologies alone are not adequate."[17] In 2001, the NGO Forum of the World Conference Against Racism supported reparations for the African slave trade.

Truth Commissions
Truth commissions are not courts, but they are official forums set up to give victims and perpetrators the chance

to provide evidence of human rights abuses. In some cases they have been successful at beginning the long process of national reconciliation.

Over twenty-five truth commissions have been established around the world since 1974. Some of the best-known commissions have taken place in Argentina, Chile,

The Guatemalan Truth Commission

As in the rest of the Americas, Spanish colonization of Central America killed off 90 percent of the Mayans between the sixteenth and seventeenth centuries. Yet in spite of being subjected to unrelenting racism and persecution, each generation of Mayans in Guatemala has fought to retain its language and culture. Today Mayans make up 60 percent of the population of Guatemala's 10 million people.

A decades-long conflict between the American-supported Guatemalan military and leftist rebels peaked in the early 1980s when the military targeted Mayan villages, destroying hundreds of them and massacring thousands of villagers whom they accused of supporting the rebels. Over a million people were displaced by the violence. In 1996, a truth commission was part of the agreement to end the war.

In 1999, the resulting Historical Clarification Commission provided evidence that over 200,000 Guatemalans had been killed or "disappeared" (i.e., they were kidnapped and never seen again). Hundreds of thousands had been subjected to barbarous torture. The commission found that the government was responsible for 93 percent of the crimes and that 83 percent of the violence was directed against Mayans. Tracing the roots of government repression against the

Guatemala and South Africa. All of these dealt with crimes against humanity; only the Guatemalan case was recognized as genocide. The commissions have generally been successful in placing long-denied atrocities on a nation's agenda and in providing important historical information, including estimates of the number of victims.

Mayans back to the sixteenth century and the Spanish conquest, the commission ruled that the Guatemalan state had committed genocide.

It was a victory that the centuries-old persecution of the Maya — and in particular the government's campaign of terror from 1981 to 1983 — was recognized as genocide. But the ruling also pointed out the difficulty of not being able to recognize the genocide of political groups. For the violence was not just directed against Mayans as an ethnic group but against Mayans as political insurgents, as well as against people from other ethnic groups, including many Ladinos (most of whom are descendants of the Spanish), who also opposed the military regime. The Mayans were not the only people in Guatemala who were fighting for land reform, basic civil rights and an end to repression.

What the ruling has meant is that Mayans are seen as victims of genocide, when many Mayans would also like to be recognized as courageous insurgents. And other insurgents are ineligible for reparations because they are not Mayan.[18] So although there are many positive aspects to the ruling, it also raises a number of problems about the use of the term genocide and what it means to describe someone as a victim of genocide.

The striking difference between the South African Truth and Reconciliation Commission and regular court cases, according to Justice Albie Sachs of the Constitutional Court of South Africa, was that "truth came pouring out" of the truth commission proceedings. The South African commission offered perpetrators immunity from punishment if they agreed to tell the whole story and admit what they had done. It also allowed victims to face perpetrators in order to encourage healing and even forgiveness. But forgiveness is not easy. For Justice Sachs, whether individuals forgave other individuals was not so important. What was significant was the massive inequality that still existed between perpetrators and victims in South Africa:

> The real problem with reconciliation is that when the killers left the proceedings, they drove off to their fancy houses with swimming pools, while the victims went off to their shacks.[19]

Bringing out the truth, acknowledging what happened, is crucial to the process of healing. But without reparations for victims and equal opportunities for them in the post-genocidal society, reconciliation is impossible.

Chapter 7
Preventing Genocide

> To prevent genocide, the most racist of crimes, the
> United Nations must enlist the whole human race.
> We will need an international movement to end
> genocide that has the size and moral force of the
> anti-slavery movement.
>
> — Gregory Stanton[1]

The information about mass killings and genocide is
there if we search for it. Human rights organizations and
activists, academics and journalists use the internet —
and to a lesser extent, television, radio and the print
media — to bring attention to the world's trouble spots.
Scholarly research is teaching us about past genocides
and providing insight into the factors that may trigger
genocide in a particular time or place. The International
Criminal Court and the Yugoslav and Rwanda tribunals
are beginning to present an alternative to the passivity of
governments and individuals standing by and allowing
the leaders of a genocide to go free yet again.

The UN World Summit declaration in September 2005 affirmed the UN's and individual countries' "responsibility to protect" (R2P) a country's citizens in the face of major violations of human rights. Hailed as an important advance in human rights law, the R2P asserts that "each individual State has the responsibility to protect its populations from genocide, war crimes, ethnic cleansing and crimes against humanity." The R2P deals with prevention of these crimes as well as stopping them once they have started. And it states that the UN, through the Security Council, is prepared to take collective action, that is, to intervene "should peaceful means be inadequate and national authorities manifestly failing to protect their populations" from these crimes.

Unfortunately, the R2P (a Canadian initiative) was watered down from its original form. The summit declaration allows the Security Council to deal with situations "on a case-by-case basis," in other words, giving it the option whether to act or not and no clear obligation to act in the face of these crimes.

To date, no government or group of governments has adequately confronted the ongoing genocide in the Darfur region of Sudan. There is no "political will" — no commitment by governments to devote the needed efforts and resources — and no mass movement against genocide that could influence politicians to make the choice (for it is a choice) to stop the genocide in Darfur.

The American invasion of Iraq in March 2003 has

undoubtedly influenced many governments' perspectives on any kind of intervention, including the humanitarian intervention (implied by the R2P) that is needed in Darfur. The ongoing commitment of American, British and other troops in Iraq and in Afghanistan also means there are fewer troops available to take part in any such intervention. It is also likely, given the non-obligatory nature of the R2P, that some states will continue to use their clout on the Security Council to argue that the situation within their borders is their responsibility alone.

Unfortunately, the situation in Sudan is just the tip of the iceberg. There are erupting genocides or politicides in many regions around the world. Genocide Watch lists twenty countries, including Sudan, where it says a genocidal process has already begun:

- in Africa: Chad, the Democratic Republic of the Congo, Ethiopia, Sudan (Darfur and South Sudan), Uganda, Zimbabwe;
- in South America: Colombia;
- in Asia: Afghanistan, China, India (in the states of Gujarat and Kashmir), Indonesia, Myanmar (Burma), Nepal, North Korea, the Philippines, Sri Lanka, Uzbekistan;
- in Europe: Russia-Chechnya;
- in the Middle East: Iraq and Israel-Palestine.[2]

Some might disagree that every one of these situations qualifies as genocide, for all of the usual reasons, including: it is not taking place on a big scale, or it is a civil war, or it is a war against terrorism. But what is clear is that systematic mass killing is not an isolated phenomenon. It is taking place in countries all over the world. And these gross violations of human rights, though they may appear to be isolated one from the other, are inter-connected.

Trace the origins of the racist ideas or the methods or the weapons used in a particular genocide, and there is always a connection to other bigots or strongmen or arms dealers, some government or corporation elsewhere that is helping to prop up or supply the perpetrators. And by supporting the perpetrators in any way, they are both encouraging them to continue their actions and implying that they can carry on with impunity, drawing in ever more and more victims.

Genocidal situations are difficult to face, but the United Nations, governments, organizations and individuals can — and must — take action.

It is in everybody's interest to prevent genocide.

First Steps

Prevention is part of the very name of the Convention on the Prevention and Punishment of the Crime of Genocide. Conspiracy to commit genocide, incitement to commit genocide and attempts to commit genocide are all crimes under article 3 of the convention.

The Genocide Convention has its shortcomings, but it is gaining strength through its use by the Yugoslav and

Rwanda tribunals and the establishment of the ICC. By the end of 2005, 137 countries had signed the Genocide Convention (50 countries, including Indonesia, Japan and Nigeria had not yet signed). According to article 8 of the convention, any of these 137 signatories "may call upon the competent organs of the United Nations to take such action under the Charter of the United Nations as they consider appropriate for the prevention and suppression of acts of genocide or any of the other acts enumerated in article 3." Excluding Sudan itself (which signed the convention in 2003) that leaves 136 countries who could call on the UN to take a stand against the genocide in Darfur, for example.

But the gears of the United Nations move into position very slowly and not without grinding ponderously before they do. As in every other human rights struggle, work needs to be done on a number of different fronts at the same time. Bringing perpetrators to trial from past genocides and ensuring that all the evidence comes out publicly and is recorded and discussed are central to helping prevent future genocides. At the same time, genocide resisters and rescuers must be recognized and rewarded, and the stories of people who risked their lives for others made public and retold, again and again.

Racism and ethnocentrism and other "us-them" ways of seeing the world are at the root of genocide. This means that genocides are less likely to happen in countries that value human rights and where the minority

Resistance and Rescuers

There has undoubtedly been more resistance to genocide and more attempted rescues of genocide victims than have been reported due to the simple fact that many people who fought back were killed. But stories of resistance and rescuers live on.

Armenians fought back against the Ottoman Turks in a number of places during the Armenian genocide. In Van, a beautiful walled city situated on a plateau close to the Russian border, 1,300 men and boys, a few with rifles and others with ancient weapons, defended 30,000 Armenians against the Turks for almost a month between April 20 and May 17, 1915.[3]

During the Holocaust, there was armed resistance by Jews, Roma, leftists and others who were not necessarily targeted, and Jews joined the underground resistance in a number of countries, including France, Italy, Slovakia and Yugoslavia. Jews fought back in the Warsaw Ghetto, and at Treblinka, Bialystok and Sobibor camps. Some people worked to spread information about the Holocaust, and others hid Jews or helped them escape. Jewish cultural resistance to the genocide — a refusal to give up even when there was no reason to hope — was also remarkable. The Vilna Ghetto (in Poland during the war and then in Lithuania), for example, had a library, a school

rights of all groups — including ethnic, religious, racial, same-sex, political and social — are protected by law. Laws against hate literature and hate media must be enforced. Individuals must commit themselves to speak out against racism, sexism, discrimination and persecution at every level — from refusing to ignore genocidal killings to refusing to use ethnic stereotypes, and refusing to participate in gay bashing or any type of bullying, system, a day-care center and weekly concerts, plays and literary evenings.[4]

Hutu peasants, local officials and church members died defending their fellow citizens during the Rwandan genocide. Jean Marie-Vianney Gisagara, the mayor in Nyabisindu, Butare, had local police arrest the Interahamwe after an attack and continued to oppose the genocide, even when he had run out of options. He was beaten and then killed by being tied to a van and dragged through his city's streets. Sula Karuhimbi, a seventy-five-year-old traditional healer and peasant farmer in Gitarama, hid people in an animal shelter and fed them with food from her fields. Ms Karuhimbi braved numerous threats but she and the people she sheltered are still alive.[5]

A study of non-Jews who helped Jews during the Holocaust identified rescuers as having the following characteristics: a strong sense of individuality, self-reliance, a history of standing up for others, and a tendency to see their aid as ordinary, and not particularly heroic.[6] The Rwandan rescuers exhibit these same qualities, including the remarkable final quality: assuming that helping others is not extraordinary, but is what anyone would do.

or even to laugh at racist, sexist and ethnocentric jokes.

It is crucial to recognize that in every place where a genocide takes place there is an historical background that has produced it, a situation that could have been influenced at any number of stages to prevent the genocide. It is therefore essential to study our own and other people's histories, and to develop a background for understanding and analyzing current situations and conflicts.

The Role of Governments

The term "political will" is often first on the list of things needed for governments to make any big, important change. It usually refers to the need for governments to commit themselves to putting in the time, effort and resources to do something. But in many ways, political will is only a euphemism for choice. Governments (and organizations and individuals) can choose whether or not to focus on halting or preventing genocide. It is a choice that may demand a big commitment, or it may only require withdrawing support to a genocidal regime. But it is still a choice.

It is no use waiting for influential governments to make a move. Small, less powerful governments can choose to begin the process to make a difference. In the case of Darfur, for example, it would mean a government deciding to condemn the actions of the government in Khartoum and demand that they stop their genocidal activities. It would involve getting support from other governments and the UN, withholding aid and supplies of arms, divesting from companies doing business with the Sudanese government and imposing sanctions. Finally, it would mean committing troops who might risk their lives to ensure that perpetrators are arrested, disarmed and immobilized. This last obligation is one of the most difficult. Although governments may be willing to put their troops in danger when they are protecting "strategic" interests, the Rwandan situation shows that

Good Cop or Bad Cop?

The United States holds a central position in any global discussion of genocide. It is the world's largest military power — some would even say the "world's policeman" — and American individuals and institutions are responsible for some of the best work on human rights over the last century.

At the same time, the US has a long history of supporting dictatorships that back US interests. It is notorious for being the only Western country that actively uses the death penalty. It is alone among industrialized countries in its refusal to sign some of the world's most central human rights documents, including the Convention on the Elimination of All Forms of Discrimination against Women (CEDAW) and the Convention on the Rights of the Child. It has not signed other essential international agreements such as the Landmines Convention and the Kyoto Protocol on Global Warming. It only signed the Genocide Convention under heavy pressure in 1988, following many attempts to "water down" the articles of the convention. (In 1950, for example, a US Senate committee tried to ensure that US treatment of African Americans would not be considered genocide by recommending an amendment to the convention to state that "genocide does not apply to lynchings, race riots or any form of segregation."[7])

Since the attacks of September 11, 2001, the US position on human rights has worsened and has had an impact on human rights in allied countries like Canada, the UK and Mexico, as well as in the rest of the world. Terrorist suspects in the US can now be held without charges for months, even years, without ever knowing the evidence against them.

American government rhetoric, describing a group of countries as "the axis of evil," for example, sounds more and more like the hate propaganda that often anticipates genocidal massacres. The US invasion of Iraq, against the protests of the United Nations, and the killing of between 35,000 and 98,000 Iraqi civilians[8] is illegal according to the Geneva Conventions, which the US has signed.

It is interesting that the US could have made a case using the Genocide Convention to invade Iraq on the basis of the Anfal genocide of the Kurds by Saddam Hussein's regime. But that atrocity took place in 1988 when the administration of US president Ronald Reagan was supporting the Iraqi government. It was only in late 2002, when the UN failed to find weapons of mass destruction, that the US talked about "regime change" as a reason for its invasion. And it didn't mention genocide.

The US resolutely refuses to join the International Criminal Court (ICC), though it continues to try to influence it. And while President Bush has called the situation in Darfur genocide, he is also on good terms with the genocidal Sudanese government on whom he relies for information about Muslim fundamentalists in the so-called war on terror.[9]

Why does the US refuse to sign these international agreements and conventions? The answer is obvious: it does not want to be held accountable (e.g., for the Convention on the Rights of the Child's commitment to a child's right to housing, or in the case of the ICC, for war crimes). It is much less obvious how to persuade the world's biggest military and economic power to use its clout to stop or prevent genocide.

governments are less likely to commit large numbers of combat-ready troops when it is "just" a situation of human rights.

The Role of Humanitarian Organizations

Non-governmental organizations (NGOs), such as Oxfam, Save the Children, Concern and other humanitarian organizations — including UN agencies such as the UN High Commission for Refugees (UNHCR), the UN Children's Fund (UNICEF), the World Health Organization (WHO) and the World Food Program (WFP) — are usually among the first to gather evidence of genocidal situations. But they often find themselves in the dilemma that once they make the situation known, they are unable to do their job. The Red Cross, for example, failed to publicize what it knew about the Nazi death camps during World War II in order to continue to support wounded soldiers and prisoners of war. One can only ask how it is possible to be neutral — which the Red Cross prides itself on being — in the face of genocide.

Some NGOs are willing to take a firm stance against genocide. In Sudan, in June 2005, for example, two doctors from Médicins sans Frontières (MSF) were arrested and held for three weeks by the Sudanese government. The arrests followed the release of an MSF report of testimony from hundreds of rape victims in Darfur. The government of Sudan was not afraid to threaten foreigners who dared to document its atrocities, but could not get away with killing them, as it does its own citizens.

Protected as they are, international organizations and citizens have a crucial role to play.

It is the job of local and international NGOs working on the ground in genocidal situations to document the atrocities and bring them to the attention of the rest of the world. It is the job of the rest of us to listen to their stories and act on them.

The Role of the Media

The media, like humanitarian organizations, are often among the first to draw attention to an emerging genocide. They too have a duty to make the situation known and help mobilize assistance to those at risk.

"You can't stop a genocide if you don't know about it," affirms the Be a Witness website at www.beawitness.org. Set up in 2005 to publicize the genocide in Darfur, Be a Witness points out that in the month of June 2005, American television stations — from which three-quarters of Americans say they get their information — devoted only 126 news segments to the genocide in Darfur. What dominated television news that month? A total of 8,303 segments on the "runaway bride," the Michael Jackson trial and Tom Cruise. Be a Witness encourages people to contact the media and tell them that genocide *is* news.

The Darfur genocide is not the first to be buried by the media. Mainstream media coverage of the Ukrainian famine, the Holocaust, the genocides in East Timor,

Cambodia, Rwanda and elsewhere was either missing entirely or hopelessly inadequate. There are many reasons, including the same reasons that governments and individuals do not take up the issue: racism, complicity with the perpetrators of the genocide, or a lack of strategic interest in the region where the genocide is taking place. The media also tend to follow other media outlets' leads. So if no one else is airing or printing stories about Darfur, they don't see the point of doing it themselves.

In addition, the insecurity in a genocidal environment often means that local reporters are silenced and foreign reporters leave for their own safety. In Rwanda, for example, four days after the genocide began, some newspapers began to report that the killing had ended. In fact, it was just that the coverage of the genocide had been halted, because most of the foreign journalists had left the country.[10] Reporters who do remain in dangerous situations often have trouble convincing their bosses that their stories deserve airtime or newspaper space.

The Role of the UN

The adoption of the "responsibility to protect" strengthens the UN's commitment to collective action against genocide and other crimes against humanity. But any relevant resolutions must still go through the difficult test of the Security Council, made up of permanent members China, France, Russia, the United Kingdom and the United States, each of which can veto any resolution that comes to the council. Members of the Security Council often refuse to act in situations in countries where they have a strategic interest. But there is still room for influence or "moral suasion," that is, persuading governments to support intervention in genocide by shaming them for standing by.

In 2004, the UN appointed its first Special Advisor on the Prevention of Genocide. Special advisor Juan Mendez is an Argentinian human rights lawyer and one-time political prisoner. It's only a part-time position and Mendez has been given few resources. But with support from organizations and individuals and a willingness to take chances, special advisor Mendez could become an important actor in genocide prevention.

Mendez sees the UN role as first, providing protection and humanitarian aid for the people at risk using UN peacekeepers, international civilian monitors and relief workers; second, showing perpetrators that they will be charged for genocide and other serious crimes against humanity; and third, working to resolve conflicts that might result in genocide.[11]

The Role of Individuals
One of the main roles that individuals can play is to mobilize political will — to put so much pressure on governments that they will have to act to change the situation. How? In the case of Darfur, for example, it could mean supporting existing organizations (see Genocide

Activists, page 135) by donating money to support their work or volunteering to help with the work, or both. It could mean spending time discussing the issues with people who are unaware of them (personal connections are always important); writing petitions and getting them signed; organizing and attending events to publicize the genocide; and putting pressure on the media to provide consistent and detailed coverage of the crisis.

Getting involved is not always easy or straightforward. It means not being discouraged by the long waits and the inevitable setbacks and the people who don't think your cause is important. It means working with people whom you may not always agree with or who do things in different ways. It may mean not receiving much recognition for your work. But if it means saving even one life, it is worthwhile.

Early Warning Systems

It is not always easy to draw a circle around a genocide — to define precisely where it starts and stops. But there are always signs of its approach, in the taking away of rights, in hate propaganda, in the building up of arms and civilian militia, in the psychological and physical separating out of an "enemy within."

Based on their analysis of the factors common to different genocides, genocide activists have developed early warning systems to help predict where and when a genocide might occur. These systems include some early indicators of genocide:

- the use of identity cards to identify specific groups;
- the absence of laws to prevent or punish discrimination against specific groups;
- the exclusion of specific groups from positions of power;
- the use of the media to demonize or dehumanize specific groups;
- the segregation of specific groups;
- the forced relocation or eviction of specific groups from land or property;
- the prevention of delivery of essential services or assistance, including blocking access to food, water, sanitation or essential medical supplies;
- the organization of militias or paramilitary groups.[12]

One or two of these indicators, while demonstrating a situation of persecution against a particular group, do not necessarily lead to genocide. Several of them would be more likely to warn of a serious human rights crisis. What is important is making potential victims, people in opposition to a genocidal government, regional and international governments, NGOs and individuals aware of the signs of a lead-up to a genocide, and agreeing on early actions to counter the potential crisis.

The Need for a Tsunami-like Response

The big-hearted worldwide response to the tsunami in South Asia at the end of December 2004 raises the issue, Why is there not a similar response to genocide? Genocide is a disaster too. Why are people more likely to help victims of a natural disaster than those of a human-made disaster like genocide? Is it because they see the victims differently?

The victims of the tsunami are completely innocent of their fate. And the victims of genocide? Although most people would not admit it (they would deny it), at some level they must hold the victims of genocide responsible for what has happened to them.

It may also be that in recognizing the tsunami victims, people don't have to face the trauma of massive deaths at the hands of other people. And they don't have to face the dark side of their fellow human beings (or themselves).

Supporting the tsunami victims does not require a search for an uncomfortable or "unspeakable" truth. Supporting the victims of a genocide — or better still, speaking up to help prevent a genocide before it occurs — does.

Genocide, like all other aspects of our shared humanity, is something we need to face head on, to think about and try to understand, not just for the sake of knowledge, but in order to prevent it happening in the future. If we are able to recognize and react to the early warning signs — the social, political and economic conditions that allow genocide to take place — we might be able to help stop it. It's worth a try. Much more than that, it's worth our best efforts.

Human Rights and Genocide Timeline

1689	English Bill of Rights
1776	US Declaration of Independence
1789	French Declaration of the Rights of Man and the Citizen
1792	Mary Wollstonecraft publishes *A Vindication of the Rights of Woman*
1914	World War I begins
1915	Armenian genocide
1919	World War I ends
	League of Nations founded
	International Labour Organization founded
	Court of Justice founded at the Hague
1926	League of Nations Convention to Suppress the Slave Trade and Slavery
1932-33	Forced famine in Ukraine in the Soviet Union
1937	Rape of Nanking, Chinese massacred by Japanese troops
1937-38	Great Terror in the Soviet Union
1939	World War II begins
1939-45	Nazi Holocaust
1943	Raphael Lemkin coins the term genocide
1944	The term genocide appears in print for the first time in Raphael Lemkin's book, *Axis Rule in Occupied Europe*
1945	World War II ends
	United Nations founded and International Court of Justice established
1945-46	Nuremberg Trials
1946	UN General Assembly passes a resolution condemning genocide
1948	Convention on the Prevention and Punishment of Genocide is passed by the UN General Assembly, the first time the UN adopts a human rights treaty (entered into force in 1951)
	Universal Declaration of Human Rights is passed by the UN General Assembly
1949	Geneva Conventions established on treatment of civilians and prisoners during wartime
1961	Amnesty International founded

1965	International Convention on the Elimination of All Forms of Racial Discrimination (entered into force in 1969)
1965-66	Genocide of Indonesian leftists
1966	International Covenant on Civil and Political Rights and International Covenant on Economic, Social and Cultural Rights (both entered into force in 1976)
1972	Genocide of Hutus in Burundi
1973	International Convention on the Suppression and Punishment of the Crime of Apartheid (entered into force in 1976)
1975	Indonesian forces invade East Timor
	UN Declaration on the Rights of Disabled Persons
1975-79	Cambodian genocide
1975-99	Genocide of East Timorese
1978	Helsinki Watch – later Human Rights Watch – founded
1979	Convention on the Elimination of All Forms of Discrimination against Women (entered into force in 1981)
1981-83	Guatemalan genocide
1984	UN Convention against Torture and Other Cruel, Inhuman or Degrading Treatment or Punishment (entered into force in 1987)
1988	Anfal genocide in Iraq
1989	Convention on the Rights of the Child (entered into force in 1990)
	Indigenous and Tribal Peoples' Convention (entered into force in 1991)
1990	International Convention on the Protection of the Rights of All Migrant Workers and Members of Their Families
1991	Civil war begins in Yugoslavia
1991-1995	Genocide in Bosnia-Herzegovina
1993	Yugoslav Tribunal established
1994	Rwandan genocide
	Rwanda Tribunal established
1995	Beijing Conference on Women's Rights
1998	Report of South African Truth and Reconciliation Commission
	First conviction for genocide – the Rwanda Tribunal finds Jean-Paul Akayesu guilty. The Akayesu Judgment also recognizes rape as a genocidal act for the first time

1999	Commission for Historical Clarification presents its report stating genocide was committed in Guatemala from 1981–83
1999	UN peacekeepers arrive in East Timor, finally ending the genocide
2002	International Criminal Court is established
2003–today	Genocide in Darfur
2005	UN World Summit agrees on "responsibility to protect" people from genocide, war crimes, ethnic cleansing and crimes against humanity
2006	Genocide in Darfur spills into neighboring Chad. Peace agreement signed between Sudan and one rebel group

Note: There is often a long delay between the time a UN treaty or convention is signed by member states and the time when it officially enters into force. Both dates are given where applicable.

Genocides through History

Genocide	Date	Victims	Number of Victims	Percentage Population
Carthage	146 BC	Carthaginian men, women and children	150,000	75%
Transatlantic Slave Trade	1450–1850	Africans (chiefly from western Africa and west central Africa, some from southeastern Africa)	36 million to 60 million	66%–75% of those captured
Arawak/Taino	1492–1650	Arawaks/Tainos, indigenous inhabitants of the Caribbean islands	250,000 to 4 million	100%
American Native Peoples	1492–1891	Indigenous inhabitants of North, Central, South America and the Caribbean	100 million	95%
Beothuk	1500–1829	Beothuks, indigenous inhabitants of Newfoundland	1,600 to 5,000 Last Beothuk, Shawnawdithit, died in 1829	100%
Herero	1904	Hereros in Southwest Africa (now Namibia)	64,000	80%
Armenian	1915	Armenians in the Ottoman Empire (now Turkey)	1.1 million to 1.8 million	50%–75%

Note: It is impossible to provide the full context for or even list every genocide here. It is hoped that readers will be inspired to follow their interest beginning with the titles suggested in For Further Reading. Historic estimates of the number of victims sometimes vary widely; in these cases, the range is given.

Perpetrators	Method of Killing	Sexual Violence	Trials
Roman soldiers	Two-year siege, starvation, disease, burning houses, swords, axes	Unknown	No
Spanish, Portuguese, British, French, Dutch slavers and citizens	Execution, torture, forced emigration and forced labor, starvation, disease	Yes	No
Spanish conquistadors and settlers	Massacres, slavery, over-work, disease (especially smallpox)	Yes	No
Spanish, Portuguese, British, French, Americans, Canadians	Massacres, torture, slavery, overwork, disease (especially smallpox), forced marches, starvation	Yes	No
British settlers	Occupation of coastal areas, depriving Beothuks of traditional food sources; torture and killing	Yes	No
German colonialists and German army	Massacres, forced marches, denied access to water, poisoned water supply, slave labor, starvation, disease	Yes	No. German apology in 2004. Hereros call for reparations in 2005.
Ottoman soldiers, militias (largely made up of ex-convicts), peasants	Massacres (mass shootings, as well as killing by daggers, swords, scimitars, bayonets, axes, saws and cudgels), drowning, burning alive, execution, torture, forced marches, starvation	Unknown numbers of women raped before being killed; some kidnapped	Some trials of leaders in absentia, so no punishment. No recognition by Turkish government

Genocide	Date	Victims	Number of Victims	Percentage Population
Ukrainian Famine	1932-1933	Ukrainian kulaks and other peasants, Ukrainian communists who opposed the genocide	7 million	25%
Nanking Massacre	1937	Chinese people in Nanking	300,000 civilians and soldiers in city	50%
Holocaust	1939-1945	Jews, Roma, Slavs, leftists, disabled, Afro-Germans, gay men	6 million Jews; 500,000 Roma; 200,000-250,000 disabled; 10,000 to 15,000 gay men	67% of Jews in Europe; 50% of Roma in Nazi-occupied Europe
Indonesia	1965-1966	Members of the Indonesian Communist Party (leftists), many identified through lists provided by the US CIA, including many ethnic Chinese	500,000	Unknown
Cambodia	1975-1979	City people, former government officials, the educated and well-off, intellectuals, ethnic Vietnamese, ethnic Thai, Cham Muslims, Buddhist priests	1.7 million to 2.2 million	21% to 25%
East Timor	1975-1999	Timorese men, women and children	200,000	30%

Perpetrators	Method of Killing	Sexual Violence	Trials
Soviet officials	Shooting, torture, starvation, forced migration to the Arctic and Siberia	Unknown	No. Apology by USSR in 1990
Japanese soldiers	Massacres, torture, shooting, burying alive, stabbings, drowning	80,000 women raped	Mentioned at Tokyo War Crimes Trial (1946-48); faint apology in 1998; full apology and reparations demanded
Nazi army, mobile killing units, special police units (SS); civilians, including doctors, business people, civil servants	Massacres, execution, gassing, torture, forced ghettoization, internment in prison camps, over-crowding, starvation, overwork	Unknown numbers of women raped in ghettos and con-centration camps and women and men sexually abused	Nuremberg Trials, 1945-1946
Anti-communist army, civilian militias	Massacres at night, but bodies were later dis-played to spread terror, bayonets, machetes, beheadings, forced imprisonment	Rape and violent sexual assault of women	No
Khmer Rouge army	Execution, shooting, tor-ture, forced marches, star-vation, overwork	Unknown	Cambodian tribunal planned
Indonesian army, militias	Land, sea and air invasion (1975-77), napalm, massacres, executions, incarceration, starvation, disease	Sexual torture and rape, kidnapping of women for use as sex slaves; forced "marriage" and sterilization	Ad Hoc Court inadequate; calls for genuine international tribunal or use of ICC

Genocide	Date	Victims	Number of Victims	Percentage Population
Guatemala	1981–1983	Mainly Mayans (83%), leftists	200,000	3%
Anfal, Iraq	1988	Kurdish men, women and children	182,000	4%
Bosnia–Herzegovina	1991–1995	Bosnian Muslims (Bosniaks)	200,000	6%
Rwanda	1994	Tutsis, some moderate Hutus	800,000 to 1 million	71%–83%
Darfur, Sudan	2003–	Zaghawa, Masalit and Fur tribes	450,000	8%

Perpetrators	Method of Killing	Sexual Violence	Trials
Guatemalan army, death squads, militias	Massacres, execution; torture including beating children against walls or throwing them alive into pits, covering people with gasoline and burning them alive; opening the wombs of pregnant women	Sexual torture and rape before women were killed	Historical Clarification Commission finds Guatemalan government guilty of genocide. Some low-level officers, soldiers and militia convicted but no senior army officers
Iraqi army, presidential guard, government officials at all levels, who were often obliged to take part in executions to enforce subservience to Saddam Hussein	Massacres, executions (100,000 men and boys machine-gunned to death), chemical weapons (mustard gas and GB or Sarin) in Halabja, burning of villages, forced displacement from homes, starvation, disease	Unknown	Saddam Hussein charged with genocide in April 2006 by new Iraqi government
Bosnian Serbs	Massacres, executions, shooting, torture	50,000 women raped	Yugoslav Tribunal (1993-)
Hutu government, Interahamwe militia, thousands of citizens	Massacres, executions, torture, throwing explosives into houses, machetes	250,000 to 500,000 women raped	Rwanda Tribunal for leaders (1994-), Gacaca trials (2002-), Rwandans charged with genocide in Belgium, 2002; in Canada, 2005
Sudanese army and air force, janjaweed militias	Bombing, massacres, burning villages, shooting, burning alive and other torture, forced marches, starvation	Thousands of women and girls raped and gang-raped and beaten with sticks, whips or axes; often mutilated	List of 51 perpetrators of "crimes against humanity" given to ICC by UN in March 2005; 4 low-level Sudanese sanctioned by UN in April 2006

Notes

1 Today's Genocide

1. Eric Reeves, "Darfur in the Deepening Shadow of Auschwitz, Bosnia, Cambodia, Rwanda," October 24, 2005. Available at www.sudanreeves.org.
2. Samantha Power, "Dying in Darfur," *The New Yorker*, August 30, 2004, 61.
3. Eric Reeves, "Quantifying Genocide in Darfur: Part 2," May 13, 2006, www.sudanreeves.org.
4. Nicholas Kristof, "The Secret Genocide Archive," *New York Times*, February 23, 2005.
5. Eric Reeves identifies some of the Sudanese government members named by the UN in "The UN Takes Its Turn at Posturing on Genocide in Darfur and Eastern Chad," April 18, 2006, www.sudanreeves.org. He notes that National Islamic Front President and Commander-in-Chief, Field Marshal Omar el-Bashir clearly should be on the list as well.

2 The Ultimate Crime Against Humanity

1. Raphael Lemkin, "Genocide," *American Scholar*, Vol. 15, No. 2 (April 1946), 227-30. Available at www.preventgeno cide.org/lemkin/americanscholar1946.htm#II:%20The%20 word.
2. Geoffrey Robertson, *Crimes Against Humanity: The Struggle for Global Justice* (New York: New Press, 2000), 3.
3. Nuremberg Charter, Article 6 (c), available at www.yale.edu/lawweb/avalon/imt/proc/imtconst.htm#art12.

4. Samantha Power, *A Problem from Hell: America and the Age of Genocide* (New York: Perennial/HarperCollins, 2002), 17.
5. Cited in Samantha Power, *A Problem from Hell*, 43.
6. The full text of the convention is available at www.unhchr.ch/html/menu3/b/p_genoci.htm.
7. David King, "Canada," in *Encyclopedia of Genocide and Crimes Against Humanity*, ed. Dinah Shelton, three volumes (Macmillan Reference, 2005).

3 A History of Mass Violence

1. Mahmood Mandami, *When Victims Become Killers: Colonialism, Nativism and the Genocide in Rwanda* (Princeton, NJ: Princeton University Press, 2001), 9.
2. Roger W. Smith, "As Old as History," in *Will Genocide Ever End?* eds. Carol Rittner, John K. Roth and James M. Smith (St. Paul: Paragon House, 2002), 31.
3. I owe this insight to Meg Luxton.
4. Frank Chalk and Kurt Jonassohn, *The History and Sociology of Genocide: Analyses and Case Studies* (New Haven and London: Yale University Press and Montreal Institute for Genocide Studies, 1990), 78.
5. Adam Hochschild, *King Leopold's Ghost: A Story of Greed, Terror, and Heroism in Colonial Africa* (Boston and New York: Houghton Mifflin Company, 1998), 225-33.
6. Thanks to Gerry Caplan for pointing this out to me.
7. David Stannard, "Introduction" to *A Little Matter of Genocide. Holocaust and Denial in the Americas: 1492 to the Present,* by Ward Churchill (Winnipeg: Arbeiter Ring Publishing, 1998), xvi. See also David Stannard, *American Holocaust: Columbus and the Conquest of the New World* (London: Oxford University Press, 1992).
8. Roger W. Smith, "State Power and Genocidal Intent: On

the Uses of Genocide in the Twentieth Century," in *Studies in Comparative Genocide*, by Levon Chorbajian and George Shirinian (London: Macmillan and New York: St. Martin's Press, 1999), 4-5.

9. David Stannard, *American Holocaust*, 317-18.

10. See Robert Conquest, "Ukraine 1933: The Terror Famine," Genocide and Mass Murder in the Twentieth Century, October 24-December 12, 1995, United States Holocaust Memorial Museum, Washington, DC; Bohda Krawchenko, "Collectivization and the Famine," Ukrainian Canadian Committee, Edmonton Branch, October 14, 1983, available at www.artukraine.com/mail.htm; Frank Sysyn, "The Ukrainian Famine" in *Studies in Comparative Genocide*.

4 Theories of Genocide

1. Philip Gourevitch, "Never Againism," *Granta* 87 (Fall 2004), 117.

2. Helen Fein, "Option Paper, Threats: Anticipating Genocidal Violence," Stockholm International Forum, 2004. Available at www.preventgenocide.org/prevent/ conferences.

3. Roger W. Smith, "As Old as History," 33.

4. Helen Fein, "Option Paper, Threats."

5. Brent Beardsley, Zoryan Institute Course on Genocide and Human Rights, Toronto, August 8, 2005.

6. See Genocide Watch website, www.genocidewatch.org.

7. According to *The Concise Oxford English Dictionary*, tenth edition, revised (Oxford: Oxford University Press, 2002).

8. Christopher R. Browning, *The Origins of the Final Solution: The Evolution of Nazi Jewish Policy, September 1939-March 1942* (Lincoln and Jerusalem: University of Nebraska Press and Yad Vashem, 2004), 247.

9. "Warsaw," in *Holocaust Encyclopedia*, Walter Laquer, ed. (New Haven and London: Yale University Press, 2001), 687. Ester Reiter brought the details of the appalling scarcity of food in the Warsaw Ghetto to my attention.

10. Mengele was a Nazi physician known as "the Angel of Death," who often took part in the initial separation of prisoners at Auschwitz, and sent an estimated 400,000 Jews to the gas chambers there. He carried out malevolent medical experiments (neither ethical nor scientific) on twins, dwarfs and others, killing most of his subjects in the process.

5 The Anatomy of a Genocide

1. Peter Novick, *The Holocaust in American Life* (New York: Houghton Mifflin Company, 1999), 221. Novick notes that there is no record of Niemoeller's first statement, in the late 1940s or early 1950s, of this much-used and often changed quotation — but this version is authorized by his widow, Else. Thanks to Roger Smith for referring me to the original citation. Niemoeller was a Protestant pastor who at first supported the Nazis, but later became openly critical of the Third Reich. He was imprisoned in concentration camps for seven years and freed in 1945.

2. The expression "words can kill" is from Herbert Hirsch, *Genocide and the Politics of Memory: Studying Death to Preserve Life* (Chapel Hill and London: University of North Carolina Press, 1995), 97. Hirsch also emphasizes the role of sexism in genocide, 102, 112.

3. Genocide Watch website, www.genocidewatch.org.

4. Gwynne Dyer, *War* (New York: Crown Publishers, 1985), 118.

5. Stanley Milgram, *Obedience to Authority* (New York: Harper and Row, 1974), 189.

6. Jean Hatzfeld, *Machete Season: The Killers in Rwanda*

Speak. Translated from the French by Linda Coverdale (New York: Farrar, Straus and Giroux, 2005), 48-49.

7. Ben Kiernan, "Twentieth-Century Genocides," in *Specter of Genocide: Mass Murder in Historical Perspective*, Robert Gellately and Ben Kiernan, eds. (Cambridge: Cambridge University Press, 2003), 45.

8. Israel Charny, *How Can We Commit the Unthinkable? Genocide: The Human Cancer* (Boulder, CO: Westview Press, 1982), 202.

9. Seth Mydans, "One Artist, One Million Memories," *New York Times*, September 7, 2002.

10. See Roger W. Smith, "Women and Genocide: Notes on an Unwritten History," *Holocaust and Genocide Studies*, Vol. 8, No. 3 (Winter 1994), 315-34, for examples from Germany and Cambodia. Dr Smith included accounts from Rwanda in a discussion at the Zoryan Institute Course in Toronto, August 9, 2005.

11. "Women's Lives and Bodies — Unrecognized Casualties of War," Amnesty International Press Release, December 8, 2004. Available at www.amnesty.org/library/Index /ENGACT770952004.

12. Andrea Smith, *Conquest: Sexual Violence and American Indian Genocide* (Cambridge: South End Press, 2005).

13. See "A Human Rights Response to Discrimination and Violence against Indigenous Women in Canada" (October 2004). Available at www.amnesty.ca/campaigns/resources /amr2000304.pdf.

14. Belma Becirbasic and Dzenana Secic, "Invisible Casualties of War: Bosnia's Raped Women Are Being Shunned by a Society that Refuses to See Them as Victims," *New Series Bosnia Report*, No: 32-34 (December-July 2003).

6 Responding to Genocide

1. Lieutenant-General Romeo Dallaire, with Major Brent Beardsley, *Shake Hands with the Devil: The Failure of Humanity in Rwanda* (Toronto: Vintage, 2003), 6.

2. See Tim Wheeler, *People's Weekly World*, October 2004, available at http://www.PWW.org and www.crmvet.org.

3. Jean-Paul Sartre, *On Genocide* (Boston: Beacon Press, 1968), 83.

4. Geoffrey Robertson, *Crimes Against Humanity*, 334.

5. The WTI held hearings around the world for two years and its Jury of Conscience, represented by Indian activist and novelist Arundathi Roy, announced its conclusions in Turkey in June 2005: "the attack on Iraq is an attack on justice, on liberty, on our safety, on our future, on us all." See WTI website: www.worldtribunal.org/main.htm and www.truthout.org/docs_2005/062705A.shtml.

6. The Office of the United Nations High Commission on Human Rights identifies seven core international human rights treaties: the International Convention on the Elimination of All Forms of Racial Discrimination; the International Covenant on Civil and Political Rights; the International Covenant on Economic, Social and Cultural Rights; the Convention on the Elimination of All Forms of Discrimination against Women; the Convention against Torture and Other Cruel, Inhuman or Degrading Treatment or Punishment; the Convention on the Rights of the Child and the International Convention on the Protection of the Rights of All Migrant Workers and Members of Their Families. See www.ohchr.org/english/law/index.htm for a list of about ninety other international human rights instruments, including the Genocide Convention, which appears under the heading of "War Crimes and Crimes Against Humanity, Including Genocide."

7. See Stephanie Nolen, "Rwanda 10 Years After: Don't Talk to Me About Justice," *The Globe and Mail*, April 3, 2004, F6.

8. Linda Melvern, *Conspiracy to Murder: The Rwandan Genocide* (London: Verso, 2004), 232.

9. Romeo Dallaire, *Shake Hands with the Devil*, 522.

10. Rome Statute of the International Criminal Court, available at www.un.org/law/icc/statute/romefra.htm.

11. Baudrillard is cited in Martha Minow, *Between Vengeance and Forgiveness: Facing History after Genocide and Mass Violence* (Boston: Beacon Press, 1998), 118.

12. Judith Lewis Herman, *Trauma and Recovery* (New York: Basic Books, 1992), 1.

13. Jean Hatzfeld, *Machete Season*, 242.

14. Ervin Staub, *The Roots of Evil: The Origins of Genocide and Other Group Violence* (Cambridge: Cambridge University Press, 1989), 150.

15. Gerald Caplan makes this point in "From Rwanda to Darfur: Lessons Learned?" *Sudan Tribune*, January 18, 2006, available at www.sudantribune.com/article_impr. php3?id_article=13601.

16. Martha Minow, *Between Vengeance and Forgiveness*, 93.

17. Organization of African Unity, *Rwanda: The Preventable Genocide. Report of the International Panel of Eminent Personalities* (2000), 266. Available at www.visiontv.ca/ RememberRwanda/Report.pdf.

18. Carlota McAllister raised these issues in her talk, "The Genocide in Guatemala and Its Aftermath," at Indigenous Struggles in the Americas and Around the World: Land, Autonomy, and Recognition, York University, Toronto, February 10, 2005.

19. Albie Sachs was speaking on "Human Rights Issues, Personal Perspectives," at the Raoul Wallenberg Day

International Human Rights Symposium, Osgoode Hall
Law School, Toronto, January 18, 2005.

7 Preventing Genocide

1. Gregory Stanton, Presentation to Stockholm International
   Forum, January 2004. Available at
   www.preventgenocide.org/prevent/conferences.
2. Genocide Watch website, genocidewatch.org/genocidetable
   2005.htm. Chad and Zimbabwe, though not on the table,
   were highlighted in April 2006 as being at risk of genocide
   and politicide, respectively.
3. Peter Balakian, *The Burning Tigris: The Armenian Genocide
   and America's Response* (New York: HarperCollins, 2003),
   205.
4. See Ester Reiter, "Book Review," *Outlook* (September
   2003), where she cites the information from Herman
   Kruk, *The Last Days of the Jerusalem of Lithuania:
   Chronicles from the Vilna Ghetto and the Camps, 1939-
   1994*, Benjamin Harshav, ed., Barbara Harshav, trans.
   (New York: Yale University Press, 2002).
5. For these and other examples from Rwanda, see African
   Rights, "Rwanda: Tribute to Courage. Summary," 2002.
   Available at www.africanrights.org/publications.html.
6. Nechama Tec, "Rescuers: Holocaust," in *Encyclopedia of
   Genocide and Crimes Against Humanity*, Dinah Shelton, ed.
7. Samantha Power, *A Problem from Hell*, 68.
8. The lower number is based on confirmed reports (May
   2006); see Iraq Body Count, www.iraqbodycount.org. The
   higher number is an estimate made by Les Roberts et al.,
   "Mortality Before and After the 2003 Invasion of Iraq:
   Cluster Sample Survey," *The Lancet*, Vol. 364, Issue 9448
   (November 20, 2004), 1857-64.
9. See Gerald Caplan, "From Rwanda to Darfur."

10. Alan J. Kuperman, "How the Media Missed Rwandan Genocide," International Press Institute Report (No. 1, 2000). Available at www.freemedia.at/index1.html.

11. Juan E. Mendez, "Ultimate Crime, Ultimate Challenge — Human Rights and Genocide," Address to the International Conference, Yerevan, Armenia, April 20, 2005.

12. Minority Rights Group International and International Movement Against All Forms of Discrimination and Racism. Joint Statement to United Nations Committee on the Elimination of Racial Discrimination, Thematic Discussion on the Prevention of Genocide, February 28-March 1, 2005; Mendez, "Ultimate Crime."

13. Melvern, *Conspiracy to Murder*, 60-61.

For Further Information

Genocide Activists

Hundreds of international non-governmental organizations (NGOs) are active in the area of human rights in general; a few focus on genocide in particular and some focus on specific genocides.

The largest and best-known of the human rights organizations are Amnesty International, www.amnesty.org, based in London, and Human Rights Watch, www.hrw.org, based in New York. Both produce detailed annual reports on human rights situations around the world, with Amnesty tending to focus on themes, such as violence against women, and Human Rights Watch on individual countries. They put pressure on governments to respond to situations like the one in Darfur. Human Rights Watch was one of the first organizations, for example, to lobby for the International Criminal Court.

A number of organizations deal specifically with genocide. They include Genocide Watch, www.genocidewatch.org/, an organization based in Washington, DC, that coordinates the International Campaign to End Genocide (ICEG), which aims to prevent and stop genocide and bring perpetrators to justice. Groups that make up the ICEG include the Montreal Institute for Genocide and Human Rights Studies, www.migs.concordia.ca/; the Institute for the Study of Genocide (ISG) / International Association of Genocide Scholars (IAGS), www.isg-iags.org/index.html; Prevent Genocide International, www.preventgenocide.org/, an Internet-based network of activists; and International Alert,

Standing International Forum on Ethnic Conflict, Genocide and Human Rights.

The Genocide Intervention Fund (GIF), www.genocidein tervention.net, based in Washington, DC, aims to increase public awareness about genocide and help prevent and stop genocide. The Aegis Trust, www.aegistrust.org, in Newark, Nottingshire, UK, does research on genocide and promotes its prevention. The Committee on Conscience at the Holocaust Memorial Museum in Washington, DC, also works to prevent genocide.

Darfur

A striking element of the opposition to the genocide in Darfur is the linking up of Jewish, Christian, Muslim and Rwandan organizations and activists. High school and university students are spearheading campaigns in many cities in North America. American English professor Eric Reeves has extensively researched the situation in Sudan and provides detailed up-to-date information at www.sudanreeves.org.

Organizations working to stop the genocide in Darfur include the UK-based Protect Darfur, www.protectdarfur.co.uk; the university student organization, Stand Canada, www.stand canada.org; the American-based Darfur Peace and Development Organization, www.darfurpeaceanddevelopment.org; and Save Darfur, www.savedarfur.org.

For Further Reading

Dozens of books, articles and websites were consulted during the research for this book. Many are listed in the notes on pages 126 to 134. The following are key texts for those interested in continuing to learn about particular genocides and the field of genocide studies as a whole.

Chalk, Frank and Kurt Jonassohn. *The History and Sociology of Genocide: Analyses and Case Studies*. New Haven and London: Yale University Press and Montreal Institute for Genocide Studies, 1990.

Charny, Israel, et al., eds. *Encyclopedia of Genocide*. Volumes 1 and 2. Santa Barbara, CA: ABC-Clio Inc., 1999.

Chorbajian, Levon and George Shirinian. *Studies in Comparative Genocide*. London: Macmillan, 1999.

Convention on the Prevention and Punishment of the Crime of Genocide. Available at www.unhchr.ch/html/menu3/b/p_genoci.htm.

Dallaire, Lieutenant-General Romeo, with Major Brent Beardsley. *Shake Hands with the Devil: The Failure of Humanity in Rwanda*. Toronto: Vintage, 2004.

Gellately, Robert and Ben Kiernan, eds. *Specter of Genocide: Mass Murder in Historical Perspective*. Cambridge: Cambridge University Press, 2003.

Hatzfeld, Jean. *Machete Season: The Killers in Rwanda Speak*. Translated from the French by Linda Coverdale. New York: Farrar, Straus and Giroux, 2005.

Lemkin, Raphael. 1946. "Genocide," *American Scholar*, Volume

15, no. 2 (April 1946), pp. 227-30. Available at www.pre
ventgenocide.org/lemkin/americanscholar1946.htm#II:%20
The%20word.

Levi, Primo. *If This Is a Man.* New York: Orion Press, 1960.

Power, Samantha. *A Problem from Hell: America and the Age of Genocide.* New York: Perennial/HarperCollins, 2002.

Robertson, Geoffrey. *Crimes Against Humanity: The Struggle for Global Justice.* New York: New Press, 2000.

Shelton, Dinah, Howard Adelman, Frank Chalk, Alexandre Kiss and William A. Schabas, eds. *Encyclopedia of Genocide and Crimes Against Humanity.* Three Volumes. Macmillan Reference, 2005.

Stanton, Gregory. Genocide Watch website, available at www.genocidewatch.org/.

Totten, Samuel, William S. Parsons and Israel W. Charny, eds. *Century of Genocide: Critical Essays and Eyewitness Accounts.* Second Edition. New York and London: Routledge, 2004.

Acknowledgments

I would like to thank my partner, Greg Keast, for his wonderful support throughout this project and for being my most inspirited reader at every stage. Thanks to Patsy Aldana for encouraging me to take on this difficult topic and for her valuable input. Thanks to Meg Luxton, Ester Reiter, Mielle Chandler and Shelley Tanaka for their excellent advice and feedback. Thanks to my son, Carl Keast, for joining me to watch many, often bleak, videos and for discussing them with such insight. And thanks to Maureen Hynes and to my mother, Peg Springer, for being there.

Gerald Caplan and Roger W. Smith provided essential expert advice with grace and sensitivity. I'm grateful to them both for helping me find my way through some of the thornier issues. Thanks, too, to George Shirinian and the Zoryan Institute for Genocide Studies for the opportunity to attend part of the 2005 Course on Genocide and Human Rights. And thanks to Leon Grek and HIC Darfur for the map on page 6.

Nan Froman, an astute reader and a gracious colleague, made the editing process a rewarding one. I'm grateful to the rest of the staff at Groundwood Books – especially Lisa Nave, Sarah Quinn and Michael Solomon – for their accomplished and good-natured assistance.

Index